All or Nothing

All or Nothing

Preston L. Allen

AKASHIC BOOKS
NEW YORK

1/08

This is a work of fiction. All names, characters, places, and incidents are the product of the author's imagination. Any resemblance to real events or persons, living or dead, is entirely coincidental.

Published by Akashic Books
©2007 Preston L. Allen

ISBN-13: 978-1-933354-41-5
Library of Congress Control Number: 2007926131

First printing

Akashic Books
PO Box 1456
New York, NY 10009
info@akashicbooks.com
www.akashicbooks.com

To Dawn, for the love that endureth

The world is the house of the strong. I shall not know until the end what I have won or lost in this place, in this vast gambling den where I have spent more than sixty years, dice box in hand, shaking the dice.

—Denis Diderot

PART I
Addicts

P's Addiction

You call your job and whisper, I don't feel good. I can't come in.

Then you shower, put on your uniform, and tell your wife, Well, goodbye, hon, I'm off to work.

Then you go gamble.

That time you went to the airport to pick up your aunt coming in from out of town, you left home three hours early so you could get a couple hours of gambling in.

Good plan.

Brilliant.

The allergic son gets sick in the middle of the night. Choking and wheezing. A stroke of luck. You tell the wife, No, hon, stay home, you need your rest, I'll take him to the emergency room. You leave your cell phone number with the nurse at the desk. You tell her, I'll be outside in my car catching some winks, please call me when they release him.

This has happened many times before. You know it takes the doctors at least three hours to treat and release him. This gives you time to get some gambling in. If anything goes wrong—flat tire, car accident, or maybe you get carried away and stay too long gambling—what's the worst that can happen? The kid is safe. The kid is at a hospital, right? Good plan.

This is a good plan?

You should be ashamed.

Shame on you.

But for a gambler it is a good plan. Shame is only temporary. No shame gets in the way.

A gambler wears all his shame like yesterday's dirt on skin. He washes it off at night and gets up in the morning ready to gamble again because today just might be the day.

2.

There was the famous no-name storm.

The no-name hurricane. It shows up on the weather map as a tropical storm. At the very worst, the weather guy says, it might make a very weak category 1 hurricane. Furthermore, it is aiming at the west coast of Florida, which is far, far away from Miami. The mayor decides to do nothing. The storm is too weak and too far away. There will be no school closings. Everything will be open tomorrow as usual. We all go to bed.

Sometime in the middle of the night, the storm strengthens and begins to move east, toward Miami. In fact, it is guaranteed to hit Miami by 6 a.m., says the weather guy. And it is a hurricane, technically, but just barely; it is a very weak hurricane. So the mayor decides, again, to keep the county running. There will be school in the morning— despite the fact that there is going to be a hurricane. Can you believe the mayor? Sending kids to school in a hurricane? In some ways, he's worse than a gambler. The mayor must be a gambler. But secretly.

So 5 o'clock in the morning, the sky is black and starless and the wind is lashing the landscape with rain. I've got my radio on as I drive to the depot. The announcers are still relaying the mayor's orders: business as usual in Miami. There will be school today. But me, I gave my wife strict orders before I left home: Do not send the boys to school in this mess; screw the mayor; the mayor's an idiot.

By the time I get to the depot, we've got flood conditions. Seven inches of rain on the ground. Trees bending from the stress of the wind. We are soaking wet in our raincoats and water boots and our umbrellas trying to fly out of our hands from the wind. The storm is sitting right on top of us now. We can hear it screaming like a locomotive. We look up into the blackness and imagine we see an eye. We run inside the depot, listen on the radio, and take bets on how long before the idiot mayor reverses his decision. It comes just before 5:45. Harry gets the pot: $12. He had 5:44. I come in second. I had 5:48. Bundled in our raincoats, we dash out to our buses instead of our cars. Lots of gas. Higher wheelbase. We'll bring them back tomorrow. Of course, I don't head home because Indian casinos stay open 24 hours a day, 365 days a year, come rain, come shine, come category 1 hurricane.

It takes me forever to get there, despite the higher wheelbase of the bus. There's so much water on the ground I can't make any better than 15 miles per hour. When I get there, the parking lot is full of cars so I have to park far from the building. I leave my school bus and try to get through the parking lot fast as I can, wading through a foot of rain. Kinda like running with boots full of water. My boots *are* full of water. Inside they have blankets waiting to dry me off, and robes to wear from their hotel rooms upstairs. It's tough to get a table because there are too many players waiting and so many of the dealers couldn't make it in because of the storm. See, it's too stormy for dealers, but the players are all here. What does that tell you? So I play the machines. I put in a lucky $20 and play for like two hours in my Indian casino hotel robe. Up, down, up, down, up. Someone jokes, They've fixed the machines to not kill us today on account of the storm. Maybe he's right. When they finally call my name for cards, I am up $120. I go to the card table and I do all right there, as well. Maybe they've fixed the cards to not kill us, too.

The storm ends around noon, and I'm still winning, but I figure I'd better leave or the wife will know what I'm up to. I surrender my Indian casino hotel robe and make my exit.

Outside the wind is gone and so is the rain. The sun is shining bright in the sky. I have never seen a bluer sky. But there is still so much water on the ground. It's like driving through a lake. There are many stalled cars on the road. Everybody on the radio seems pissed off at the mayor for not shutting things down sooner. With all of that water on the ground, it takes about an hour to get home.

The wife says, Where have you been?

I tell her, I was stuck in it. What a mess it was. Can you believe that idiot mayor made us go to work in this?

They said on the TV that they canceled school, she says.

Yeah, but when we got the news, we had to go back to the schools and pick them up all over again and take them home. What a mess. We had to wait around to make sure they were all accounted for.

The mayor is an idiot, she says.

Yes, he is, I agree.

Then I go into the bathroom to count my winnings. It was a good day, though I could have been killed.

I am up $300.

3.

There was the time one of my ATM cards started acting up.

You would slide it through the little slot in the machine, and it would give you an error message—*CARD NOT READ*. You had to hold your hand just right to get it to work. You had to have a steady hand to make it work. Then, after a while, not even a steady hand was good enough. It was crazy. The fickle card would pick which ATMs it wanted to work in, and it would work in none other. Sometimes the magnetic strip starts acting up like that and you have no choice but to contact your bank and order a replacement card.

Wouldn't you know it? The ATMs that mine chose not to work in were at the Indian casino. The damned card will work everywhere except at my favorite place in the whole wide world.

So one night I'm playing and I run out of cash. I have already burned through the one bank's ATM card that is working and hit my daily limit there. I pull out the bad ATM card from my other bank, the replacement for which still hasn't arrived. I pray to God because I need this cash to get me some luck to get me back even. I try the steady-hand method like ten times, but no luck—all I'm getting is *CARD NOT READ*. Then what I do is, I leave the place and jump in my car and drive to an ATM machine at a grocery store about a half hour away where the fickle card usually works. When I get there, sure enough—it works fine. I withdraw the money, then drive back to the casino, lose that, then get in my car and drive back to the distant grocery store's ATM and do it again, and again, and again, until my daily limit is reached on that card, too. Then I go home.

The next day, when I hit my daily limit on the good card, I am about to drive to the distant grocery store's ATM when I witness a miracle. There is a gambler at the casino's ATM with the same problem I have—a fickle ATM card—but she has solved it. She has wrapped her card's magnetic strip in the cellophane cover of her cigarette pack, and using a steady hand, has gotten it to work.

Stupid me. Why didn't I make this connection before? I have seen cashiers in grocery stores do this trick many times when a customer's ATM card doesn't work.

When the gambler ahead of me at the ATM has finished, I ask to borrow her cellophane cover. She hands it to me and laughs, Good luck.

Eureka. It works. I am able to draw out the money. I am back in business.

When I lose that, I draw out some more.

When I lose that, I discover that somehow I have also lost my cellophane wrap, so now I go searching on the ground and picking through the ashtrays and garbage bins until I find another magical, mystical tossed-away cigarette pack wrapper. Again the cellophane trick works.

It keeps working until I have hit my daily limit. I do that all week until my replacement card finally arrives. What a neat trick. Yep.

4.

Sick. Sick. Sick, you must be saying to yourself. P, you are sick.

Yep. Yep. Yep.

5.

I hear gamblers say, How did I get in this mess? One day I'm a normal guy, the next day I'm mortgaging my house to fund my gambling. It all happened so suddenly.

That is a damned lie. It never happens suddenly. No one had a gun to your head. No one had a gun to my head.

I could have done well in school, but school was not my thing. I liked school, just not a lot. My favorite subjects were social studies and language arts—I was pretty good in language arts. In junior high I wrote a poem that won a prize, and then they sent it to the *Miami Herald*, where it got published. That was kind of cool. Sports? I was good at basketball. In football, I could take a hit and give a good one, too. I'm not so tall, but I am heavy in the chest and legs. I never played on any school teams—too much discipline for me. I preferred the pickup games at the park or on the street in front of our three-bedroom house in the Carol City section of Miami, the middle-class neighborhood where I grew up in the late '70s and early '80s.

I was a normal kid. I had an Afro when Afros were in style, and by the time I graduated high school in 1980, I was wearing my hair cut low to the scalp with rows of tight, greased waves cultivated by hours of arduous brushing and nights of sleeping in a wave cap (i.e., a cap made from pantyhose I swiped from one of my sisters).

After school was over, I took a few courses at the community college. I had this brief dream that I would go into aviation, but like I said, school was not my thing, so I quit after one term. I made all Cs. I joined the Reserves. I got my union card and worked as a longshoreman with my father for a while. The money was pretty decent, but I needed more of it, so I got a part-time job as a security guard at the courthouse. I saved up enough money from working the two jobs to buy my first car, a '79 Buick Electra 225, what we used to call a deuce and a quarter. It was a nice ride to go cruising in with the fellas—what was left of the fellas, now that so many of them were in college or the military or shackled to a wife and kids. So that was how I spent my weeks—working my two jobs Monday through Friday, then chasing women with the remaining fellas on the weekends. I met that first stupid girl and got her pregnant. I was a baby daddy. That was kind of cool. All in all, it was a good life, though it ended kinda quick. The next thing I knew, I was married, with kids, another kid from that first stupid girl (court-ordered child support), and a mortgage.

But that was a good life, too. I loved my wife and kids. I devoted myself to being a good father, which wasn't difficult to do because I had come from a good home with a good father—he was quick with the belt, especially when he drank, but overall a good father, who could always be counted on to bail you out or kick some toughness into you, whichever you needed.

I buckled down and learned how to juggle the bills. But they were *bills*, and I never learned how to like them. Everything cost so much, I discovered. My friends were starting to acquire things—material possessions—that I could not. I would see them in their BMWs. Or with their large houses. I began to see the limits of what we could have as a family because of my limitations as a provider. I did not let it show, but there was some guilt there. Maybe I should have tried harder in school, for my family's sake. Maybe I could have been something better than what I was.

But what I was, was a regular guy.

What was wrong with that?

I refused to succumb to jealousy. I comforted myself with a thing that was clear and true: We lived good. There was nothing wrong with the way we lived. Other people may have had more, but we lived good. We certainly didn't live bad.

My wife was a bridesmaid at her friend's wedding. The friend, who had never been married before, was in her mid-30s at the time. Both she and the groom were doctors. It was a fabulous affair, held at one of the grandest hotels in Miami, the Biltmore. My wife was more beautiful than all of the bridesmaids and the bride, too. To put it nicely, the bride was not a cute woman—she is my wife's dear friend, so no offense, but she is zero in the cute department. I mean, she has this nose job that's so bad it makes her old ugly nose look good. So you know how it is, my wife and I got to cracking up about it that night in bed.

My wife said, But the dress. Did you see the dress? You have to admit the dress was beautiful.

And I said, Yes, hon, but did you see who was wearing it? That nose. Who is she trying to be, Michael Jackson? Forget the dress, she needs to work on getting the rest of her nose back.

And my wife said, That dress cost more than you make in a year.

This hurt a little bit, but I did not let it show. I said to my wife in the dark beside me, Ha-ha, but to still end up looking like that after spending all that money on a dress. Ha-ha.

My wife said, All that money? All *what* money? In the real world, that is not a lot of money.

We had a house in a decent neighborhood, we had two big-screen TVs, we had two cars, we were raising children who had all the newest toys and bikes, we went on a two-week vacation to my sister's house in Atlanta once a year. We made it work. We knew how to juggle. We lived good. We had love. We had quality of life.

But in the real world, *what I made* was not a lot of money.

What I made was less than what her not-cute friend the doctor spent on a dress she would wear only once.

If that was the real world, what world was I living in?

My wife is a good wife. This was the only time she ever said anything like that about money, about where we were in life, and after she said it, she became quiet. Real quiet. I was quiet, too.

Then my wife reached out, found my hand, held it tight, and began to talk about the Christmas gift she had picked out for my parents that year (this was before my father had died). I mumbled my agreement, though I was not really listening to the particulars of what she was saying. That she was even saying it was the proof I needed that she still loved me.

Even though my money, in the *real world,* was not a lot.

But a bus driver does live in the real world. Casinos are in the real world, and a bus driver, sitting there with all those jackpots, those blinking lights on those machines, dreams about the day when he's got more money than any not-cute doctor that his wife went to high school with. Sure, he may have made a few errors along the way. Sure, he could have done better.

But a casino can fix all errors and right all wrongs.

All it takes is one push and the slate is wiped clean.

All you have to be is lucky.

6.

It was Super Bowl Sunday, and I was seeing 7s and 9s.

Everywhere I looked it seemed that 7s and 9s were popping up. Billboards. License plates. Dollar bills. And always in groups of four, with the 7s leading the 9s.

A few years ago, I held a contract for 7-9-7-9. Played it for four months, then decided it was a dud and stopped playing it. Just to spite me it came in like the very next day. I never got over that. So I knew it was God talking again. The 7-9-7-9 was finally ready to come back to me. This time I would catch it.

I was doing okay for money at the time because I had hit a few months back, big money, *which I will tell you about later*, but it was slipping away fast. I was lying to everybody about it. All my friends thought I was still rich—I mean, I had really hit it big, but by Super Bowl Sunday more than half of it was gone. A cousin was asking to borrow money and I was willing to give it to her, but the way it was slipping through my fingers, I really couldn't afford it. The way I figured it, I needed at least $25,000 to build my account back up and still have a couple thousand to lend my cuz so I could look big in front of her. So that Super Bowl Sunday I played 7-9-7-9 in the Play-4 for eight dollars straight. If it hit, and I was certain that it would, I would take home 40 grand. Nice.

That evening, as we were watching the Patriots beat the tar out of the Panthers, the nightly numbers ticked across the bottom of the screen.

7 . . . . . 7 . . . . . 9 9

Damn.

7.

My wife screamed because she had heard me singing about 7s and 9s all day. She knew I had bought the tickets. She knew I had bought a bunch of them. The problem was that I had played it *straight* 7-9-7-9, rather than *box* 7-9-7-9, which would have covered any combination, including 7-7-9-9. I had played eight dollars straight hoping to get 40 grand. I had been so certain that I did not box it, not even once. If I had boxed just one ticket for a dollar, it would have paid $800 because the numbers were doubled twice. Instead of forty grand, or even $800, I had a pocket full of very close (very, very close) losers.

With my wife bragging to everybody about the bunch of tickets I had hit and surmising about the big bundle she assumed I had won,

I had no choice but to go into my dwindling funds and lend little cuz the couple thousand she was asking to borrow (with no hope of her ever repaying). And my wife went on another shopping spree because I couldn't admit to her that I had not boxed it even once.

So now I have two stories to tell. When I see my gambling friends, I show them the very close losers from Super Bowl Sunday and they are amazed and commiserate with me as only fellow gamblers can.

When my wife is around, I tell it different:

"Don't go letting everyone know about it. I didn't hit it straight, you know. It's not all that much. Yeah, I hit it boxed. Six or seven times. Eight hundred dollars a ticket. But that's not really a lot of money."

That's how it is with gamblers, especially the lucky ones. They expect us to win all the time, so we've got to have two stories. We've got two stories for everything.

Mom

8.

My mother believes that God talks to her in numbers, but I'm not sure. She is not a gambler, but she is the only person I know who hit the Cash-3 and Play-4 in the same day and got five numbers in the lottery that weekend.

She called my house that night whispering, "What does it mean if you have 5-4-8?"

"It depends, Mom. Is it a dollar-play or 50-cent-play? Is it box or straight?"

"Straight," she said, "for a dollar."

"Congratulations, Mom. You just won $500."

She whistled a thanks and hung up.

She called back minutes later. "What does it mean if you have 1-1-3-8?"

I said, "Mom, what's going on?"

"I just want to know."

"You're telling me that you have 1-1-3-8 straight?"

She said, "I think so. Oh, I don't know. I'm not sure how you play these things."

"Well . . . if you played it for a dollar and it says *straight* on it, then you win $5,000."

"They pay you so much?"

"Yes, Mom."

"For each ticket?"

"Each?"

"For all the ones that I bought."

"What does it say on them?"

"Well, on one it says *fifty cents* and one says *dollar*. And another one says *b-x*. What does *b-x* mean?"

"That's *box*."

"How much does that pay?"

"Usually $200, but since 1-1-3-8 has a double number in it, you get $400."

"For each ticket?"

"Mom, listen to me," I said, concerned. "How many tickets do you have?"

"I don't know. I have to see how many the lady at the grocery gave me."

"With the same number?"

"They let you play more than one number?"

"Mom, wait there. Don't call anyone, don't talk to anyone, don't do a thing until I get over there, you hear me?"

"You're coming over?"

"I'm coming over. Don't show those tickets to anyone until I get there."

I shot over to her house. She had two dollars and fifty cents straight on the Play-4, which was worth $12,500. She had three dollars on the Cash-3, which was another $1,500. I forgot how many boxes she had, but that was another bundle. I had never seen such a thing.

"This is amazing. This is incredible. Mom . . . how did this happen?"

"The old lady I work for made me go buy her ticket and her gro-ceries today. So I bought her groceries and her tickets, then I got some for myself. I used to see your father doing it all the time. Now I'm all the time watching the old lady do it. I used her numbers. And the grocery lady said, Is that all? And I said, What else can I play? She said, You can make up your own numbers. So I said, Well, just play the numbers on this check the old lady gave me. And she said, How do you want me to play them? and I said, Play them how everybody else plays them, I don't know. And she said, Okay. She really was a sweet little girl. Okay, she said to me, but for how much? And I said, Well, I have nine dollars left over from cab fare. Put all of this on it and play it the way everybody else plays it, I don't know. And the girl gave me all of these tickets."

She opened her hand.

"You put nine dollars on the same two numbers?"

"Did I do wrong? I won, right?"

I squeezed her hand. Squeezed the tickets in her hand. "Mom, you're rich!"

"Well, that's good. Now that your father's gone I could sure use the money. His pension's not much."

"Mom, you're amazing." And she was.

She forgot to tell me that she had purchased one more ticket at the suggestion of that nice girl in the grocery store.

The lotto ticket that hit five out of six numbers on Saturday night.

Another $3,200 for the lady who doesn't gamble. Another phone call to her dutiful son.

"So, you mean they're going to pay me $3,200 for one ticket by itself?"

"Yes, Mom. $3,214.64."

"I should have bought more than one ticket like I did with the others, huh?"

"You did fine, Mom."

"I did fine. You're going to come over and help me cash it in again?"

"Yes, Mom."

Beginner's luck. $3,214.64. Nice. But it wasn't fair. What about guys like us who do it all the time? Yes, I admit it, I was jealous of my own mother.

It just wasn't fair.

9.

A couple months earlier, about a year after my father had died following years of battling diabetes, my mother sank into a deep depression about loss, grief, and lack of money.

They had been together well over 40 years. He had been a longshoreman for most of their marriage and then a security supervisor at the Turkey Point Nuclear Power Plant before becoming bedridden. She had been a nurse's aide for a while, but then went back to doing day work in the homes of the wealthy Miami Beach ladies. Throughout most of their marriage and the raising of three kids, my father had taken care of the bulk of the bills. He had been the provider. My mother had worked only if she wanted to. Now she couldn't sleep at night, all the time worrying about what would happen if she couldn't pay her bills. She feared she would lose her house. She feared becoming homeless. We—my two big sisters and myself—told her that she had nothing to worry about. We would always be there for her. As a flight attendant, an elementary school music teacher, and me a bus driver, none of us were rich, but we would pitch in, we assured her, to make sure our mother was taken care of.

"It's not the same," she told me one morning, like 3 o'clock in the morning. I had just snuck back in the house from gambling late at the casino. I had told my wife that I had been hanging out with a friend and she had been grilling me about the smell of cigarettes on my clothes and accusing me of selfishness and meanness because I lacked the common decency to at least call when I planned on staying out late, and what the hell about work, didn't I have to get up for work in just a few hours?—when my mother had called. Saving me.

"It's not the same," she said. "Your father I could depend on. Oh, he was a son of a bitch sometimes, but he was my son of a bitch. You kids have your own families. I don't want to be bothering my children. I promised myself that I would never become one of those parents who pester their children."

"You don't pester us, Mom. We love you. We'd do anything for you." I turned to my wife, who was propped up on a pillow with her arms folded across her chest, breathing in a huff, eager to resume the fight. I tried to drag her into it with my mother to distract her. "Right, hon?" I said to my wife. "Mom is not a pest, right, hon?"

My wife turned her back to me and breathed a loud, indignant, "Harrumph."

I told my mother, "She said you're not a pest, Mom. See? We all love you." I smelled it then. My wife was right. I did smell like smoke. I reeked of smoke. And my pockets were stuffed with ATM receipts. I had dropped close to two grand that night, plus some cash that I already had in my pocket from checking the seats on the bus that day. The kids were always losing money in the seats. You dig around in there, you can always find a couple bucks. Some days you can find almost 10 bucks rooting around in those seats. You need every penny you can get when you gamble because when you are losing you have to spend it all. If someone says, Buy some medicine for me with this $20, my life depends on it, and you go to the casino, you will blow all of your money, blow all of the money in your ATM up to the daily maximum, then dig around in your pockets for whatever spare change you have remaining, and blow the $20 your friend gave you, whether his life depends on it or not. You will leave with nothing. Every penny you have must go into the machines because you never know when lady luck is going to dance with you. Tonight, I blew all of my loose cash, blew my daily max on the ATM, then went out to the car and found three quarters and 26 pennies in the toll tray. That made a dollar. That was all I needed. I ran back into the casino, found a floor person to turn the loose change into a paper dollar for me, and I dropped that bad boy into the machine and played it one quarter at a time, which gave me four pushes. The next thing I knew I had turned that lone dollar into $20, then $25, then $40, before my luck ran out. Now my total was counting down like a rocket ship ready for takeoff. I was down to $20. I said to myself, I *am* going to leave here with $10 in my pocket. And that wicked machine kept losing and losing. It was so frustrating. How could a machine that had turned one single dollar into $40 not hit something in 20 straight pushes—25, 26, 30 straight pushes? When it got down to nine dollars, I said, I *am* going to leave here with five dollars. At three dollars, I said, I *am* going to leave here with two dollars. At least I will have doubled my money. At two dollars, I started playing it one quarter at a time again. Eight pushes later, I left the casino with no money and absolutely no way to get any. I had hit my daily ATM maximum and the day was only about two hours old.

If you're going to be a gambler, here is what you've got to learn: The worst time to go to a casino is an hour or two before midnight, which is what I had done. See, if you hit your daily ATM maximum, which for me is $1,000, all you have to do is wait for midnight and the system resets itself. Now you are able to withdraw another $1,000, which is what I had done. Two grand in less than four hours. Smelling like smoke. Driving the car on E because I have no money for gas, through local roads because I have no change even for the turnpike tolls. Late getting home to the wife. Fighting with the wife. Lying to the wife. So sleepy it feels like sand is in my eyes, but I have to get up in about an hour and a half to get to the depot early so I can sneak on the other drivers' buses and dig around in the seats for cash the school children lost so that I'll have a few bucks to put gas in my car until my ATM limit resets at midnight. I did this to myself. I did *this* to myself. I am a gambler. A gambler is more asshole than head. A gambler is more asshole than heart. I'm an asshole. I have no head and no heart. "I love you, Mom. We all love you," I said to my mother.

"But I've been having these dreams," she said, "about numbers. I want you to write them down and play them. When you hit that million in the lotto Saturday, you can have it. I'm too old for it. I want you to have it because I know you'll take care of me."

"Numbers?" I said.

"Yes. I saw them as bright as day. You know, I used to have dreams as a child and then things would come true that I dreamt about. You need to write these numbers down and then you'll be rich and you can take care of me when you hit the lotto."

I said, "Okay," and turned to my wife. "Hon, you got a pen and paper?" Her back was still turned to me. She did not answer. I told my mother to hold the phone and I dug around on the bureau until I found a pen. I used the back of one of my ATM receipts as the paper. "Okay, Mom, I'm ready."

And my mother began to tell me these numbers.

"3."

"Okay."

"5."

"Okay."

"76."

"Mom, 76 is too high. The lotto doesn't go up that high."

"Well, you do what you can with it. I'm just giving it to you as I saw it in the dream."

"Okay."

"43."

"Okay."

"46."

"Okay."

"2."

"Uh-huh. Okay."

"46."

"Mom, you said that one already."

"34, 24, 54, 12, 13."

"Mom, that's too many numbers. You can only play six of them."

"11, 26, 36, 17."

"Mom . . ."

"31, 42, 35, 36, 37, 38, 39, 40, 41, 42."

I stopped writing. And sighed. Then started thinking of someplace new that I could stash my ATM receipts from my wife. I couldn't throw them away. I had to keep them in case I hit something big so I could show the IRS how much money I had lost as a deduction. The ATM receipts themselves are a deduction. The fee is around two bucks a pop. You take your money out in increments of 40 and 60 because you're lying to yourself about how much you're going to spend. You do that 15 or 20 times a day, you're talking 40 bucks a day just in ATM fees. You're talking four to five hundred bucks a month in ATM fees alone if you visit the casino, let's say, ten times a month. Then the bank charges you an additional monthly fee for using a non-network ATM machine. The ATM fees are a great deduction in and of themselves *if* you file your taxes, which you don't because you're too ashamed to admit that this is what you are. Sometimes you get clairvoyant and you see where all this is leading. Sometimes you think it's God talking to you. Sometimes you cling to your desperate hope as your mother keeps on reciting the bright-as-day numbers from her dream.

"46, 63, 64, 25, 36, 76, 77, 9, 10, 19, 46 . . ."

Ah, Mom.

10.

There are only two kinds of gamblers: the lucky and the broke.

For years I was the broke kind.

No matter how little money I had, I found enough to gamble, though other things, like bills and whatnot, went unpaid.

So much for a credit rating.

I took the kids to Disney because there was a casino up around there that I wanted to try out. So here I was, leaving boy number one in charge of boys numbers two, three, and four so that I could sneak off to some casino. Keep in mind that funds were limited at the time. Keep in mind that the kids were all minors. Boy number one was only 15, but he looked 18. They made out okay, had fun, didn't get lost. They stuck together. They stuck to the budget I set for them. They stuck to the conspiracy: Don't tell Mom.

Me? I lost my shirt at the casino. I had to borrow from what the boys had left over for gas money home.

A couple months later God blessed me and I became the other kind of gambler. The lucky kind.

I had always been a fan of the Rams. I'm not so into sports betting, but I had a friend in Vegas, F, I used to send a hundred bucks to every year to put on the Rams to win it all. The Rams were good back in the '80s when they had Dickerson. Then they fell into a pit of mediocrity and ineptitude for more than a decade. I still dutifully sent my hundred bucks every year to F in Vegas. In 1999, the Rams got religion and started beating everybody. By the end of the season they had the best record in football thanks mostly to the right arm of Kurt Warner and both legs of Marshall Faulk. The coaching genius of Dick Vermeil had a little something to do with it also. To make a long story short, the Rams were 150-to-1 underdogs to win it all when I bought my annual ticket back in June, and here they were in the Super Bowl, which they won. I cashed in a ticket for $15,000. My bank account had never been so happy.

That started it for me. That was also the year I hit my first royal flush at the casino poker tables. The minimum you get for that, besides the pot, is $1,000. If you hit a royal with a jackpot attached to it, you can make 20 or 30 times that much.

So I went from being a broke gambler to being a lucky gambler. The other kind. Everybody wanted to tap my stack for luck. Everybody wanted to borrow "lucky" money from me so they could catch some luck of their own. All the dealers and pit bosses knew my name. I was getting free drinks and free hotel rooms. Things like that. The dealers all wanted to deal to me so that I could hit something and tip them big. The pretty female dealers were flirting with me, though I had no interest in that kind of action at the time. That would come later, after I had really hit it big. But right then, all I wanted was to keep on gambling and keep on winning, which I did.

The wife was happy. She had money to shop and pay bills. I was happy. I had money to gamble.

If I wasn't addicted before that incredible year, that was when it happened. It was a real good year. I never thought it would end.

I never thought it could.

My mother says what I did wrong was I should've listened to God. "I think God was trying to tell you," my mother says, "Take the money and run, you damned fool."

Ah, Mom. You just don't understand gamblers.

DEGENERATES

I used to be a heavy gambler. Now I just make mental bets.
That's how I lost my mind.

—Steve Allen

ii.

This other guy, let's call him the professor. You rarely see him play. He hangs out at the slots and he cheers you on, sometimes. Sometimes he lectures you. Though he can be annoying at times, we let him get away with it.

He says, "Gambling is illegal in Florida, right? So what is this? What are we doing? We are not gambling—we are playing scratch-offs. That's right, scratch-offs. If you look at your tax receipts whenever you win, you will see the words *Winner of video pull-tab jackpot*. The implications of this are interesting. You think that you are playing a slot machine, which implies random numbers are falling, and random numbers will win. It only looks like that on the surface. What's really happening is that you are electronically scratching off on electronic scratch-off tickets. See? No? Okay, look at it like this: I purchase a scratch-off ticket in the grocery store. The ticket says I have a one-in-a-million chance of winning $100,000, right? But what if the winning ticket is up in Orlando? You see? I can scratch off all of the tickets I want down here in Miami, and I will not win because the winner never made it down here. In other words, the winner was printed and sent somewhere—could be here, could be there, could have fallen out of the bag and into the garbage can—scratch all you want, but you cannot win. Now, since these are video scratch-off games, what does that mean? It means that when the computers were programmed, a winner was designated, a winning machine, a winning hour, and a winning minute of the day. If you are not playing on that machine, at that time, on that day, you cannot win. The winner has already been determined. The numbers you put in are just an illusion to make it fun and keep you playing. People are superstitious about numbers, so the programmers put in numbers, but they could just as easily have put in signs that say *You win* or *You lose*. It's all the same thing. Now, if these machines were truly random, as they most certainly are not, every machine, potentially, could hit at the same time. Think about it. If we all flip a quarter, isn't it possible that all of them might land on heads? Yes, because the coin flips are random and independent of each other. But not these machines . . ." On and on he goes. He really is more fun when he's cheering us on. "Yes! Yes! Hit it. Take some money from these gosh darn Indians. Yes! Come on, baby, hit those sixes."

He's even more fun when he's handing out hundreds.

You'll hear him behind you: "Come on, man, those sevens have to play. They have to. Come on."

You'll say, "They're killing me today. They're beating me like a drum. I'm down to my last dollar."

He'll say, "Don't worry about it, friend, I got you covered." And he'll open his wallet and slide you a hundred.

The professor doesn't discriminate. He gives to black, white, Latino, Chinese, men, women, gays—it doesn't seem to matter. As long as you let him yak without telling him to shut up, you have a good chance of him sliding you a hundred. He's a smallish white man, youthful in appearance, but severely balding. He is always immaculately dressed in a pressed shirt and pressed pants. Sometimes he wears a jacket and tie. His shoes are always shined.

I've gotten a peep inside his wallet on several occasions. It's nice. He has a wad of hundreds in there, but he rarely plays, and when he does, he quits if he doesn't hit something after the first twenty. Such discipline is enviable. One day he watched me go to the ATM ten times before he stopped me. He said, "How much did they beat you for today, friend?"

"Professor," I said, "they beat me bad. I'm down $900."

Putting his hand on his chin to mull it over, the professor said, "That's quite a bit. Hmmm. What if I gave you $500? Would you go home right now? The only reason you continue to play is to make back the money you lost. You are tired, broke, and you probably need to be somewhere else right now. You probably have more important things to do. Do you have kids? A wife?"

"Yes, sir."

"You should be home with them. It's almost midnight." He took the $500 out of his wallet and placed it in my hands, then closed my fist around it. "Take this. You don't owe me anything. Go home to your wife and children before midnight. Go home before you hit that ATM again and do more damage to your finances. Do you hear me?"

"Yes, sir. Thank you."

"And don't let me see you in here again tonight."

"Yes, sir. Thank you. I'm going home."

"And don't go to the other casinos. If you do, and I see you there, don't even look my way again. I'm done with you."

"I won't do it, sir. I'm going home right now. Thank you."

He shook my hand. "Well, good night."

And that was it. I went home. I didn't want the professor to be done with me. I felt like a child chastised, but I went home. I was tired. I was broke. All things considered, I could have been more broke. I went home and slept next to my wife, sparing my finances from further damage that night.

The professor has a different game he runs with women. Women had better watch out for the professor. A lot of them know his deal, but some of them don't. He has a room he rents out on a nearly permanent basis in the two casinos he hangs out at the most. He is rich. He used to teach math or science or something like that at one of the local universities, until he hit it big in Vegas. The story is he won like $10,000,000 in the Vegas slots, and then proceeded to give half of it back before he did two very wise things: one, move back to South Florida where the stakes are lower; and two, join Gamblers Anonymous.

Now he has his gambling somewhat under control. But he still cruises the casinos, lecturing, bailing people out, and inviting desperate women upstairs to his room.

"Pussy is an addiction, too," the professor says. "And it's cheaper. I'd rather be addicted to pussy than gambling. When you do it to a woman, it's the same thing. It's all about the rush. It's all about the seduction. Can you get her to do it? Will you succeed with her? Will she buy your line? But what are you doing? I mean, what are you really doing? You see a pair of legs, or a nice set up top, and you go all ga-ga. Why do you feel a need to seduce her? You're the one who's going to be doing your best to pleasure her, and what do you get out of it? One quick orgasm near the end. It's not logical. They should be trying to seduce *us*. We're the ones who give, they're the ones who receive, and yet it is we who pursue them. It should be the other way around, I tell you. But, oh, we feel so good when we do it. Our self-esteem soars. Just like in gambling."

On and on he goes.

This Haitian woman, let's call her R, didn't know the professor's deal. He would cheer her on or lecture her, like he did everybody else. But instead of sliding her the random hundred-dollar bill, he would slide her three or four hundred at a time. Hmmm.

R was cute. She was short and stout with bright skin and pretty eyes. She loved the attention the professor paid to her. She certainly loved his money. She was quite the little flirt. It didn't matter that she was five or six months pregnant. Her stomach was huge, but it did not detract from her beauty.

One day R hit rock bottom—she blew close to three grand. When I got there, she was on her cell phone with her husband, trying to explain. She was frantic and crying; he was roaring back at her in an angry, deep-voiced Haitian Creole that rumbled out of the phone. The professor just stood by watching. Waiting.

R went to him and asked for money, and we all gasped.

Everybody knew better than to ask the professor for money. He never gave money when you asked. He only gave money when he felt like it. He might give a lecture when you asked. He might tell you he had no money on him, which was always a lie, when you asked. He might walk away from you shaking his head sadly when you asked. But if you are a pretty, pregnant, caramel-skinned Haitian woman he has been desiring, he might take you by the hand, look you in your honeycomb-colored eyes, and say, "You know, I have a room upstairs. Come upstairs with me. Perhaps you need to rest. Get yourself together. We'll talk about money later," when you ask.

Perhaps R needed rest. Perhaps R needed to get herself together.

But she did follow him to his room upstairs.

There are women, his regulars, who have told of the things that take place upstairs in the professor's room. He's not a really bad man. He's gentle, we are told, but very persuasive. And, of course, the woman always desperately needs the money. She will shower with the curtain pulled back so that he can watch. She will wear the assortment of lingerie that he has selected for her. He has a complete wardrobe of lingerie in all sizes. The woman gets to keep the lingerie, of course. The woman, when she hears the extraordinary sum that he is willing to give her, will dance for him in the lingerie to the disco music piping from his CD player. She will pose for him on his bed in the lingerie—and out of the lingerie, too. The woman, in desperate need of the money, will, most often, after seeing the pile of money that he will bestow upon her, select a condom from the professor's vast collection and lie with him in his bed as man with wife. It has never been reported exactly how much money the professor gives the desperate women, but they often return from his room and play the machines for hours on end, feeding hundred after hundred into the greedy, greedy things.

After that day, the Haitian woman, R, became a regular visitor to the professor's room upstairs. She never had to worry about money anymore. With the professor watching her back, she could have all the fun she wanted.

Then they had a falling out of some sort. He wouldn't talk to her. She wouldn't talk to him. These things happen. As time went on, the professor changed his mind and he wanted to make up, but R would have nothing to do with him. She didn't need him anymore because she had recently hit a big jackpot of her own, $20,000.

She told him to buzz off, and he didn't talk to her for a while, and everybody thought it was over. But one night R was playing the machines, when the professor came up behind her. He is reported to have whispered, "The truth is, I think I love you, R. I just want to love you."

She whispered back urgently, "Get away from me, you fool. My husband's here with me tonight!"

Before the professor could slip away, there was a heavy hand on his back.

"You!" R's husband roared.

The big, dark Haitian man spun the little professor around with ease.

R dropped her head into her hands, expecting the worst.

R's husband said to the professor excitedly, "You! Shame on you! Ha-ha-ha! What are you doing in a place like this, professor?" Then the big Haitian man said to his wife, "Honey, this is my old professor from college! He taught me in college, can you believe it? Honey, cash out, I want you to meet this guy. This guy is great!"

What was the poor pregnant girl to do? She had no choice.

At the insistence of her husband, R cashed out and shook hands with her lover. Then the trio, led by the big, black, joyously cackling husband, went to the casino's bar to talk about old times over drinks.

Quite a few of us at the machines knew what was really going down, so we snickered a little bit, but we didn't let on. Gamblers don't like that kind of trouble.

Furthermore, the professor was our hero. We wanted to be just like him when we grew up.

12.

In general, you're pretty safe at a casino. The owners make sure that no car thieves, pickpockets, muggers, and other assorted bad guys make an easy target of you. It happens, yes, I know it happens, crime is every-where these days, but I have watched security escort a longtime dealer off the premises—fired and banned for life—for stealing 35 cents from a customer. I have seen little old ladies with wads of hundred-dollar bills in their frail hands. Get too close to them, and security is on you in a split second. I've lost my wallet, ATM cards, hard cash, and jewelry at various times in a casino and had them all returned to me safe and sound. No problem. Casino owners protect you because you are their cash cow.

Yes, I know, there was that woman who was killed a few months ago after leaving a casino. Someone followed her home, hit her across the head when she got out of her car, and took the $4,000 in cash that she had won that night. She died, and for a few weeks the media made a big deal about how careful you have to be when you leave a casino after winning.

Maybe they're right. Maybe they're wrong. I'll tell you this: I think that lady getting smacked in the head and dying is a fluke. It says more about what kind of crime we have in Miami than how dangerous winning money at a casino can be. Are they crazy? People sometimes walk out of a casino with a $100,000 and nobody smacks them across the head.

I mean, well, it is kind of unsafe to walk around late at night with several thousand dollars in your pocketbook. I'm no fool. When I win big, I always ask for a check. The casinos will pay you up to $10,000 in cash if you ask for it. They're hoping that you will put it right back into the machines before you leave—and I've seen this happen. I've seen people win like five or six thousand dollars, take their winnings in cash, put it right back into the machines, and lose it all back. Not me. I like mine in a check.

One morning, I hit a coverall for $5,000, and I asked for it in a check. The woman working the floor misunderstood what I said and brought back a thick wad of bills to pay me off. It was still early morning, like 5 a.m., and I had 50 hundred-dollar bills bulging my wallet. As I left the casino, two young guys came up and tried to bum a few bucks from me. I told them no and instead of going to my car, I went back into the casino. I just didn't feel comfortable. To kill some time, I went back to the machines and I put a few bucks back in—lost it, of course—then I waited until the sun came up before I went to my car. I drove straight to a grocery store, since it was a Sunday morning and my bank was closed, and I bought five cashier's checks for about a thousand dollars each, drove to my bank's ATM, and deposited the cashier's checks. I felt better after that. In retrospect, I don't think the young guys who approached me outside the casino had been planning to rob me, but it had spooked me a little bit.

You have to be careful when you're carrying around that kind of cash, and that's one of the problems with gambling—you forget the value of money. You think, Five grand? That's no money. Who would steal five grand from me?

Gamblers lose all perspective on the value of money when they are in a casino. Money is a toy to us, something that we play with. It's not real like it is for most people. Money only becomes real again when we leave the casino and we have to buy a hamburger or gas up the car. We can't believe how expensive everything is—because, you see, it is our gambling money that we have to spend to buy gas, and we don't like to spend our gambling money on anything but gambling. It's weird. We'll blow thousands in a casino and think nothing of it, but afterwards drive from station to station to find the cheapest gasoline.

I don't know about other casinos around the country, but down in South Florida the most dangerous thing you will encounter in a casino is one of the syndicates, or teams of gamblers, who occupy a bank of machines when they think it is about to pay off a jackpot.

I didn't even know the syndicates existed until I bumped into one on a 24-hour binge. My wife and kids were out of town at a church retreat, so I was free to indulge. The machine I was banging was paying and taking it back and paying, and before I knew it a full day had passed. In my mind, my machine was hot, so I was focused on that and not much else. I missed that the bank of machines had filled up and that every machine was taken and that everybody was playing the MAX BET, $20 a pop. I was still playing for a quarter, and sometimes raising it up to 50 cents, or maybe a dollar. Finally, my machine went cold as it always does eventually. After surviving for a full day, I went from $500 to three dollars in ten minutes. As soon as I got up to go to the ATM, a little Chinese lady plopped down in my seat.

I said, "Excuse me, but I'm playing here. See? I still have money in the machine." I pointed to my screen, which read, $3.

She got up from my seat, very upset and muttering, "But you only playing for quarter. Everybody else playing for jackpot. You wasting seat."

What? How dare she say that? I have no problem with the Chinese, even though they are the worst degenerates in the world—I mean, they are sick—you see them all over the casino, every casino. They spend hours on the machines, they hog the machines. They seem to have unlimited money, and they're always winning the jackpots. Every time you look around, a Chinese man or woman is winning. There are so many Chinese in a casino. There are hardly any Chinese in Miami, but go into a casino and they're all over the place. In fact, half the dealers are Chinese. How is that possible? It's crazy. Like I said, I have no problem with the Chinese, but I took offense at the lady's attitude and retorted,

"It's my damned seat. I play how many damned dollars I want."

The Chinese lady rolled her eyes at me, then turned to another woman standing near her and said, "Go tell the doctor."

The doctor? I had no idea what she was talking about. I went to the ATM, withdrew another $40, and then came back to my machine, where I found the doctor waiting for me.

He was a tall, elegant man with intense eyes and smooth black skin. He looked like someone who should be wearing a top hat and white gloves and sporting a gold-tipped cane. When he spoke, his accent was African. I later learned he was Nigerian. He said to me, "Hurry and finish."

I had been there a whole day. I was hungry, sleepy, grouchy. I was miffed some Chinese woman had tried to snatch my seat. My mood was foul. Shit, I grew up in Carol City. You don't wanna mess with me. My first impulse was to send my fist through his teeth. But I didn't get a chance to because the doctor walked away. Lucky for him, I thought smugly.

When I finally ran out of money and had to leave my machine, I hooked up with the professor, who explained it to me: "The doctor runs a syndicate. When the jackpot gets up to like $150,000, he gets his team to come play the machines. He keeps them supplied with money until one of the machines hits. Then he gets 50 percent of the payoff. It costs him like 20 grand, but he stands to make 80 to a 100 grand when he wins—and he *will* win if everyone on that bank is on his team. But if there are other people playing that bank, even one other person, then his money is not guaranteed. The poor bastard just spent 20 grand for nothing. Be careful, the syndicates'll hurt you."

"Is this legal?" I asked. "Does the casino know about it?"

The professor said, "They sure don't do anything about it. There are at least four syndicates that work this casino. The doctor, the dentist, the plumber, and the Russian."

"The Russian?"

"That one owns a car dealership. You play here long enough and you'll see them all. Just be careful."

Whatever.

I don't have time to worry about that when I'm gambling. I am the bus driver. I am a syndicate of one. If the doctor, the dentist, the plumber, or even the Russian wants a piece of me, they know where to find me.

If I can brave a hurricane, I can brave some damned syndicate.

I'm from Carol City.

When I finally left the casino, I found that someone had spray painted a giant black X on my car door. When I looked at it carefully, I made out a smaller letter in front of it, R.

Rx.

With all the security cameras here, how could this happen?

At any rate, I got the message. This was my "medicine" from the doctor.

It really pissed me off, but after that I paid the proper respect to the syndicates. I would get up when they told me to get up and go to another bank of machines. Carol City boy or not, I didn't need that kind of trouble.

I just wanted to gamble.

A Gambler's Prayer Is Answered

13.

You want to be a gambler? Here's what you've got to learn: Cards have no value and no memory.

And yet I kept on getting the stinking unsuited 3-7 in Texas Hold'em. Like the good, patient player that I am, I would toss that garbage away as soon as I caught it.

But the thing is . . . see, the flop kept turning up 7s and 3s.

One time it hit 3-3-7-7, and people are winning with ace high, or ace-king, and I was kicking myself, thinking that was my freaking hand and I folded it. If I had just played the 3-7, I would have won that hand with a full house. Sevens full of 3s. It was really starting to bother me.

But you can't give in to that kind of erratic thinking.

So, disciplined player that I am, I got up from the table and got a hot dog from the café. Cleared my head. When I came back to the table, I'm catching these 3-7s again, tossing them, and they would have won if I had kept them. Frustrating. So I said to myself, Screw discipline, let's go with instinct.

The next time I caught a 3-7, I kept it. I got beat.

I caught it again, kept it, and got beat again.

In the next hour, I was dealt 3-7 like six more times, and I kept it every time, and I got beat every time, which is what is supposed to happen when you play with crap like that. You're supposed to get beat. The odds of winning with crap like that are freaking impossible. So I went back to my disciplined card playing. I tossed every crappy 3-7 that I caught.

And every time I tossed it, I would have won had I kept it.

Like I said, it's frustrating. There are days like that.

There are too many days like that.

Then there are days when you keep catching ace-king or ace-ace, and you bang the board, raising like crazy, and you lose every time. You know how it is when you play against chasers. They don't understand the game. They don't know that they should fold. You've got aces, so you're beating them on the flop. You're beating them on the turn. But they catch you on the river. Then they're so apologetic when they see what you had. They tell you that had they known how good your hand was, they would have folded. They tell you all this as they rake in the big pot they caught with the weaker hand (a 3-7, for example) that improved enough to beat your ace-ace or ace-king. Damn chasers. You just want to strangle them. They ruin the game with their erratic, inelegant play.

In Texas Hold'em, ace-ace is what you pray to have in your hand. Pocket aces. Pocket rockets. Bullets. Give them to me all day long, brother! I'll take them. You're probably going to win if you have the aces in your hand. But if you can't get pocket aces, then you want ace-king. In Texas Hold'em, we have a special name for ace-king. Big Slick we call it. It is big and it is slick, and it wins most of the hands that it is in, especially if it is suited. But there are those days when it doesn't win at all. There are those days when the chasers keep killing you.

There are too many of those days.

You begin to question God. How can there be a God if a hand like this can lose?

Like I said, cards have no value—until the last card is dealt.

And cards have no memory; just because some chaser got lucky with a crappy hand ten times in a row does not mean that it will happen for you. Cards can't remember that far back.

Cards can't remember at all.

Only gamblers can.

Gamblers remember every good hand they had that lost. Gamblers remember every penny they've lost. Gamblers remember every penny they could have had if they'd never started gambling in the first place.

14.

You get to seeing that certain numbers are linked.

For instance, in the build-your-own-lotto machines, 7s seem to come with 3s or 9s. And 9s come with 8s or 7s. Threes come with 7s or 2s. Twos come with 6s or 3s. Fours come with 6s. Fives come with 8s and sometimes 0s and 1s, but not often enough to invest your money in it; don't play 5s with 0s or 1s unless you're eager to lose your money.

If you play these machines long enough, you will see that I'm right about these pairings. This "coincidence" occurs on every machine in every Indian casino in South Florida. The same pairings. The problem is trying to figure out when to play them.

I'm sitting there playing 9s and 8s and suddenly it comes up 9s and 7s. That's not nice.

Then I move to 6s and 4s and it comes 6s and 2s. I hate when they tease me with the Off Pair like that.

One strategy is to ignore the machine and keep on playing the numbers you have. Sometimes when you do that, they send the Off Pair at you like five or six times. It will come 6-2, then 6-2-6-2, then 6-2-6.

Then sometimes 6-2-6-2-6, which is a bummer because if you had been playing it, you would have made a minimum of $450 on a quarter play.

One day, the Off Pair kept coming and I ignored it and then it came, 6-2-6-2-6-2—a coverall—minimum payout is $5,000 for a quarter play. That is not nice. Not nice at all. That has happened to me too many times to count. That is the only thing that will send me home, or to another casino. When they do that to you, you know that the camera is on you and they're up there in the control room sending you the Off Pair just to make you miserable.

I'm not being paranoid. Think about it. I'm playing 6-4-6-4-6-4 and the machine hits 6-2-6-2-6-2?

They're watching me and laughing their asses off upstairs.

The other strategy works sometimes, but be careful because it can drive you crazy. The other strategy is to switch to the Off Pair when they keep teasing you with it. The problem here, of course, is that as soon as you switch to 6-2, they will send the Old Pair, 6-4, at you. Sometimes they'll send it in big like 6-4-6, or even 6-4-6-4. Now you're thinking of how much money you could have had if you had not switched your number. Now what do you do? Switch back? If you do, then they'll send the Off Pair at you again . . . 6-2-6. The bastards. Oh, they are up there laughing at you now.

The only real good option when they're upstairs playing the Off Pair/Old Pair prank on you is to stop playing. Take your money out. Switch to a new machine. Or even better, take a break for a few minutes. Go eat something. Go play poker. Go take a pee. Then come back later and throw the Old Pair at them. But some nights, when the casino is crowded, it's difficult to find an unoccupied machine. If you leave your machine, you're stuck not playing at all for the rest of the night. So you're left with the choice of playing with a prank machine or not playing at all. If you're a gambler, you have no real choice. You have to play. You have to do it. You have to put every penny you have into a machine that you know is going to drive you crazy as it picks your pockets clean.

You sit there thinking about your empty pockets. Your empty bank account. The lie you are going to tell your wife. You think about where you can get more money to gamble so you can get some of the lost money back.

If you are going to be a gambler, here is what you have to learn: Gambling is the most addictive addiction of them all because there is never a reason to stop.

If you are winning, then you want to win more. Your seat is hot. Who wants to leave money on the table?

If you are losing, you have to get your money back. You can't leave. You can't.

If you leave, it's only to get more money and return.

If you have enough money, let's say infinity gazillion dollars squared, you will stay at the machine forever. They will find you a week later, dead from starvation, facedown on the machine. Your finger will be glued to the *PLAY* button.

This is not a bad thing.

This is every gambler's dream.

What a great way to go.

15.

Some people are crazy. They play the quick pick.

They don't believe that numbers are linked.

These are the same people who probably believe that there's no one upstairs controlling the numbers. Teasing you. Taunting you. These are the ones who just hit the QUICKPICK button and let her rip. Sometimes they hit jackpots, and I hear them say, "It was a quick pick. I just couldn't think what number to play. Oh, it's all random anyway. One number is as good as any other," and I just want to kill them. Quick pick. You just go ahead and push the QUICKPICK button and see how fast you lose your money. Go ahead and play quick pick if you're eager to go broke. Luck is not random. Luck can be studied and learned. You can make friends with luck.

There are the people who believe in playing solid numbers. All 6s or all 0s or all 9s. 6-6-6-6-6-6. 0-0-0-0-0-0. 9-9-9-9-9-9. You get the picture. I used to be one of them. They hit like that sometimes, too. They hit like that a lot, actually, but I don't trust it. You play all 6s and it comes all 3s. You switch to 3s and it comes all 7s. They will drive you crazy like that.

No, I had to give that up. I was going crazy. I started watching the machines. I began to see the patterns. Sevens with 3s; 6s with 4s; 9s with 8s. Like that.

I noticed something else, too. No one, or scarcely anyone, was playing it like that.

I started thinking, Now see, 7-3-7-3-7-3 just came up on that guy's machine and he's playing all 7s, and that's when it hit me. The game is rigged. The Indians can't have people hitting the machines all the time. If they send out numbers like 6-6-6-6-6-6 and 5-5-5-5-5-5, the odds are pretty good that almost every time they launch it, someone somewhere in the casino will hit.

They have to send numbers that excite people in order to keep them playing, but at the same time they have to be numbers that almost no one is playing.

I watched the machines and I saw the patterns, not just at one casino but at four. It was the same thing no matter where I was. All the local ones are like that. Sevens with 3s or 9s. Nines with 8s or 7s, and so on.

The first time I hit, it was a coverall on 7s and 3s—$5,000 for a quarter play. The second time, I hit on 3s and 7s. $5,000 again for a quarter play. Then I hit countless First-Fives—9-8-9-8-9_, 7-3-7-3-7_, 7-9-7-9-7_, 6-2-6-2-6_—for a variety of amounts ranging from the minimum $450 quarter play to the big $3,600 two-dollar play.

My biggest hit ever was with 2s and 3s.

I'm sitting at the casino on a bad day. They have beat me until I'm the drum. My ATM receipts are thicker than my wallet. I put in my last $20 and she bumps it up to $100. So I play her big, 10 bucks a pop. The next thing I know I'm down to like $20. I say what the heck—they always do this to me. This is crap. I give up. I swear I will never gamble again (for the hundredth time). This casino is for the birds. Why do I do this? Why do I come here and spend a thousand dollars a day? If I have a thousand dollars, why not put it on Cash-3 or Play-4? If I put it on Play-4, I have a one-in-10,000 chance of winning $5,000. If I just *randomly* put it on Play-4, I have a one-in-10,000 chance? Then what am I doing here playing this one-in-*ten million* con job? At least the state lottery is legitimate. This place is run by Indians. This place is rigged. This place is a scam. These people are Indian givers.

By this time I am talking out loud, as we sometimes do. The lady next to me is banging her machine and nodding her head in agreement. "It's a rip off," she says. "Why do we do it?"

"Because we are sick," I answer.

"Because we's gamblaz."

"You got that right."

"Why not just mail the Injuns a check? It'll save on gas comin' up here."

"Why not just burn our money? We can use it to cook when they turn off our electricity."

"You still got electricity?"

"Yeah. But no water."

She chuckles. "Why don't the Injuns just set up direct deposit and take it straight out our paychecks?"

"Why don't they use needles and suck it straight out of our veins?"

"All the money we dump in this place. They should give us somethin'."

"When are they gonna give some of it back?"

The lady looks at me and smiles. She's an older lady with a dark, cheerful face. Late 60s. Gray hair in a bun. A simple dress. Plump like a church lady. She resembles my mother in that way. She has no business being in here, I'd like to think. Gamblers come in all forms, but only two types: the lucky and the broke. She looks like the broke kind. There's a lot of that kind around here. Too many of that kind.

"Excuse me, sir," the church lady says to me, freeing her finger from the *PLAY* button for a brief second to point out something on my screen. "Why you playing 2-3-2-3-2 . . . 4?"

She's right. On my screen I have 6-2-6-2-6-2, 2-6-2-6-2-6, 3-2-3-2-3-2, and 2-3-2-3-2 . . . 4. Somehow I accidentally brushed the screen and changed the last digit. Gamblers are quick to notice patterns.

"Thank you," I say to the observant lady, and I touch the screen, resetting my number to 2-3-2-3-2 . . . 3. Then, in resignation—because I am depressed, because I have been here too long, because I am tired of smelling like cigarette smoke, because it is time to go home and lick my wounds again—I hit the *MAX BET* button, $20 per push.

Then I press *PLAY*.

(Why not give it all back to them in one push? Love me or leave me. I'll be sitting at Gamblers Anonymous tomorrow anyway. Goddamned Indians. Give some of it back!)

The balls roll across the screen one by one in magical brilliance.

2 . . . 3 . . . 2 . . . 3 . . . 2 . . . . 3!

"Nice."

"Holy-holy-holy-Lord-God-Awmighty," the lady next to me shouts above the joyous music of victory piping from my suddenly blinking machine. *Ping-ping-ping-ping-ping!* "The Injuns done paid you back!"

I feel my stress level fall for the first time in what seems like years, though it has only been two weeks. The truth is, two weeks ago I hit $6,998 in a royal flush. Since then I have sunk close to $8,000 into these machines. But this one is different. This one is a MAX PAY. This one is a hundred grand. One hundred thousand dollars. Say it with me, brothers! This one is the big payday I have prayed for. Thank you, Lord. Not even a gambler like me can blow this one. "To hell with the Indians," I say, pumping the air with my fist. "I'm rich!"

Ping-ping-ping-ping-ping!

I push the beggars away (gamblers are such beggars, always asking for "lucky" money when you win), but I tip $500 to the floor person who cashes me out then brings me the IRS form and the money ($98,000 in check, $2,000 in cash), and I lay $500 on the church lady because if she hadn't caught my mistake when she did . . . I hate to think about it. I tip $50 to the bathroom attendant, who warns, "Now sneak out of here before someone tries to rob you." I tip $50 to security for walking me out to my car. I'm rich. I'm rich. I can't believe how rich I am. This is more than triple what I make in a year even with seniority, working permanent overtime duty, working field trip duty, and my two permanent part-time jobs driving tour buses on weekends and doing security every other night at the nuclear power plant—all of which I have done and still do to make enough extra money to fund my gambling.

I'm rich. I'm rich. I'm rich. See? I told you these numbers are paired. Threes with 7s; 9s with 8s; 6s with 4s; 2s with 6s; and good-God-Awmighty, 2s with freaking 3s!!!

I'm rich. I'm rich.

Now I can pay all of my bills. Now I can pay all of the people I owe. My big sisters. My pastor. My supervisor. The eighth-graders from the afternoon bus. Now my wife can be treated the way she deserves to be treated. Like a queen. Now I can take care of my ailing mother. Now I can come to the casino anytime I like and play for as long as I like. Oh, what fun I'm going to have. I'm rich. I'm rich. I can gamble without guilt. I can spend days at the machines if I like. I can run my own syndicate if I want. I'm rich.

I have so much money they can never take it away.

HORSE SENSE

Horse sense is the thing a horse has which keeps it from betting on people.

—W.C. Fields

16.

(A Joke)

A shabbily dressed guy walked up to a casino entrance one morning and greeted a dealer just getting off the night shift. He said to the dealer: "Brother, could you spare a 20? Things are tough. I need money for food and gas."

The dealer was a compassionate guy, and he was about to reach into his wallet and give the guy the money, but then he said: "Wait. I recognize you from in there. You're a gambler. If I give you this 20, you're just gonna go inside the casino and blow it all gambling."

The gambler exclaimed: "Oh no! You're wrong. Money for gambling I got. I just need money for food and gas."

Well, that's the joke. Ha-ha.

But ain't it the truth? We always got money for gambling. We drive around in ragged cars, dressed in the shabbiest clothes, we go days without bathing or shaving, the roof at home is leaking, the light bill is unpaid, the cable is shut off, the phone is turned off, we have a regular account at the CashMyCheck store; at the CashMyCheck store they call us by our first names, we buy groceries on what credit cards aren't maxed out, we buy Christmas gifts a week late on clearance, we buy Valentine's and birthday gifts at the 99-cent counter at the drugstore and write in the card, *It's the thought that counts*, we can't afford wrapping paper, we can't afford premium unleaded, we can't afford the toll, we can't afford to rotate the tires, we can't afford auto insurance, we are hungry and we can't scrounge up four quarters for a small order of french fries—but money for gambling we got.

17.

So I hit a MAX PAY for $100,000. Good for me.

That was October.

But like I said, by Super Bowl Sunday I had eaten through more than half of it. The Patriots beat the Panthers. I lost some money on that one, too. What do I know about sports betting?

When the well runs dry, it runs dry fast.

All that money . . . man, it was fun while I had it.

Heck, I still had a lot of money.

Heck, with close to fifty grand in the bank, I still had more money than I ever had before.

Heck, if you win a hundred grand, the least you can do is risk half of it to win more, right? Are you crazy? Why not? You *don't* want to win a million?

By summer I had gone through three quarters of it.

18.

(A Definition of Insanity)

My son has magic powers.

He used to be allergic, but not so much anymore. He's kind of outgrown it, but sometimes there's a relapse. What happens is you get comfortable with that situation and then one day he's wheezing again and his eyes have rolled up in his head so only the whites show.

Now it's after midnight and I have just gotten home from the casino and there's almost no gas in the car and no way to get any because I have maxed out both my ATM cards. I'm watching the needle fall past E as we speed through the nighttime streets. My wife is in the back holding the nebulizer against his mouth. I'm praying, Don't run out of gas, don't run out of gas. We get him there without running out of gas, and they take him from us. This time it's bad. He's slipped into a sort of coma. He's like this going on 45 minutes as they work on him. I'm thinking the worst, and my wife is saying it out loud, something about strawberry cupcakes over and over. She told him never to eat strawberries, but he wants to prove to everybody that he's a big boy now and that he has outgrown his allergies.

Then one of the nurses shouts *Hallelujah!* and he's coming out of it. His chest has stopped heaving. His breathing is back to normal. The doctor is nodding his head and smiling. My son is smiling weakly.

He opens his eyes and speaks: "9-0-8."

Or maybe he says, "I'm okay." I don't know. His voice is low and swishy with phlegm. My wife thinks he said, "I'm okay."

I heard: "9-0-8."

Just to be safe, the next day I play it every possible way—straight, box, front pair, back pair. I have to borrow money from the kids on the bus to play because my ATM cards are burnt up for the next 24 hours due to my late-night visit to the casino. From the kids on the bus, I collect 16 dollars. That's good for four dollars each way.

That night the 9-0-8 hits.

I win close to three grand.

I am not surprised at all. This is the same son who when he was real young used to ride around with me and write down the numbers that he saw on billboards and license plates. I hit like that quite a few times, too.

So now I am good for a few days. A week. A month.

A month and a half later, the losing begins to hurt again as I continue my downward plunge. Nothing is hitting. Nothing. And I'm kicking myself. If I hadn't blown so much money at the casino that night, I would have been able to put a bigger wad on my son's magic allergy numbers the next day and that would have made up for the big MAX PAY I won and then blew—*am* blowing.

Day after day, I'm hopeful. I'm watching my son for signs of a relapse. He stays strong and the losing continues. One day, I find myself dragged to the grocery store by my wife. I find myself in the produce aisle fondling strawberries. Am I actually contemplating making my own son sick?

What am I?

Insane.

Say it again.

Insane.

I put the strawberries down.

My son shows no signs of relapse. This time, he's outgrown it for sure. Everybody is happy, especially him—until the night he brings the empty carton of strawberries into our bedroom. We freak. My wife is already on the phone dialing the hospital.

"I ate them all," my son says, smiling wide, "and I don't feel a thing."

He is eleven and a half and skinny and protesting, but my wife has him slung over her shoulder and is running out to the car with him.

When we get to the hospital, the doctor is waiting, but there is no reason to wait. My son explains to him, "They were tasty."

The doctor checks him with a stethoscope, then hands him a lollipop and hands us a prescription for a dose of his medicine, for just in case.

My wife and I decide that one of us should stay up and watch him through the night just in case. I volunteer.

After a while he says to me, "Why are you in here with me, Daddy?"

"Because you might get sick."

He gives me the look. He's got long lashes and bright brown eyes. This is the son I could never fool. He's the baby, but he's smarter than all the rest of them. He knows me in a way the rest of them don't. He remembers how it was driving around with me and writing down those numbers. I decide to be honest with him.

"Because you're lucky. You bring me good luck."

"I want you to be lucky, Daddy. What do I have to do?"

I shrug. "Nothing."

I couldn't say to him: *All you have to do is get sick and go into a coma, Son. Then come out of it and tell me tonight's Cash-3.*

"What's lucky about me?" he asks.

"Everything," I tell him.

He says, "Everything is lucky about me."

"Yeah. And I'm lucky to have you."

He falls asleep with me rubbing his head. He does not wheeze at all. But everything *is* lucky about him.

The next day, I play his birthday, his weight, his age, his Social Security number, every way possible in the Cash-3. I put $10 on each combination. Altogether, all the possible combinations at 10 bucks a pop set me back close to $500. Then I think about it, go back and draw out another $500, and put that on it, too. Now I have 20 bucks a pop on every possible combination. If I hit, I will be rich. No guts, no glory.

That night, the Cash-3 comes in 9-0-8 again.

That, of course, is the one combination I had not played.

Insane.

Say it again.

Insane.

19.

Yes, Lord. Yes.

What I'm trying to do now is, I'm trying to win some of it back. I learned my lesson, Lord. I won't do it again. That was too much money to blow. That was the heights of irresponsibility. A gambler is more asshole than head, but that was going too far. A hundred grand . . . oh my God oh my God oh my God, I had a hundred grand . . . I'm trying to get it back so I can do right with it this time. But it's not working. These Indians, they're not paying me anything. They've tightened up the machines or something, I know they have. They have a camera on me again. They know I won and they're trying to take it all back. I know that's what it is. It has to be. How do you spend over $75,000 and not hit anything big even once, Lord? People right next to me are hitting jackpots all day like crazy. My numbers are coming up on other people's screens. Chinese people. Why are they letting the Chinese win? Why aren't they letting the numbers come up on *my* screen? How does that happen unless it's fixed? I'm no fool. They're mocking me. A woman gets off work, she's still in her waitress uniform, she's got no shoes on her feet, she takes the machine right next to mine and hits 20 grand on the first push—she wasn't expecting to win, just dropped by to relax a bit after work, she doesn't even have her ID so they can pay her off—she has to come back tomorrow with her ID, but to me it's paying nothing. I wish I were Chinese. I wish I were a barefoot waitress who just got off work and came to a casino to relax. I *have* my ID!

I'm such a fool. They suckered me in with that big win . . . but I have a new strategy. I'm playing it small these days. No more than a hundred dollars a day. The hardest walk is the walk to the door, but I will leave every time they take a hundred dollars from me. I promise. In fact, I will leave my ATM cards at home. There will be no way for me to get more money even if I want to. I will give it to them small and sparingly, I won't go chasing Off Pairs. They will give some of it back. They have to. And this time when I hit, I'm going straight to Gamblers Anonymous to get my head straight.

I promise, Lord. I promise.

Lord.

CROSSING THE LINE

20.

E.V.
She was the pretty girl back when I drove the 262.

The 262 was a sweet gig, the rich children of Key Biscayne whooping it up about nose jobs and designer handbags. Gucci was big back then. Mine, the driver's, was the only black face on the bus, but that was okay. They were great kids, and it was a sweet route made even sweeter by the presence of E.V., the blond-haired, blue-eyed cutie pie who would become that year's homecoming queen. She would win the thing hands down. She had it all—tall, skinny, the perfect smile. She was gorgeous.

E.V. was smart, too. I would hear her back there explaining calculus to the football player she was dating. She had been accepted at Harvard or MIT, I forget which one—but she sure was a dream. She always sat near the front; I came to know her perfume. *Wings*. She was soft-spoken, thoughtful, and well-mannered. She always said goodbye and thank you when she got off the bus. She had this way of covering her mouth with her hand when she laughed. She had these innocent blue eyes—when she looked at you, you felt she was really *looking at you*.

She had legs on her, too. I would glance up in the mirror and see these two pretty knees pressed together and wish, just wish. For a while there she wore a Band-Aid on one of those pretty knees for something that happened on the volleyball team. I would love to have seen her play volleyball. Don't they play volleyball at the beach in bikinis? E.V. had such a nice tan you'd think she was something other than white. She spent a lot of time in the sun. That tan looked good on her. That blond hair.

Ah, E.V.

A couple years later, I started seeing her at the casinos. She remembered me, her bus driver. She would say hi and make small talk. She was still polite, still soft-spoken, still put her hand over her face to hide her mouth when she laughed. She was usually there with some guy—the guy would change a few times over the years—but the guy, whoever he was at the time, was always tall, good-looking, well-mannered, and rich. She would play the machines while the guy watched. She was even married to one of these hunky young guys for a short while, I came to learn. Then I started seeing her in there more frequently and unaccompanied. She was changing. She was losing weight *and* her tan, but never her manners. She still said hi to me, her old bus driver.

One night, when I was down on my luck at the machines, $20 suddenly appeared over my shoulder. I grabbed the bill and then turned to say thanks to whoever was my angel tonight.

It was E.V.

It turned out to be a lucky $20, as I recall. The thing just kept on winning until it hit FIRST FIVE—it only paid $700, because I had been playing it for a mere 50 cents.

E.V., who at that point still smelled nice, gave me a big hug for congratulations, and when I cashed out and tried to give her back the $20, she said, "Let's have drinks instead."

Let's have drinks, she said, not *Buy me a drink*. Calm down.

So we're drinking. She's downing daiquiris and I'm doing Pepsi—I like to stay sober when I gamble—and she's filling me in on her life. She never finished up her studies at college, her dad's business went under, he took his own life, her mom remarried, to a bum who ran off with the rest of the money, and her mom's most recent new man was nice, though not rich, being that he was a recent immigrant from Cuba, from whence they had all come. This surprises me.

"You didn't know I was Cuban? Really?" She laughs and covers her mouth with her hand. "We chopped off the –ez at the end to sound more American. Like Bob Villa? He's Cuban, too, you know."

"I think I heard that somewhere."

"And the hair?" she says, twisting a strand. "Dark brown."

"I would never have guessed. What else is there about E.V. that I do not know?"

"Lots," she says, and proceeds to fill me in.

E.V. herself is recently divorced, and also recently engaged—she shows me the ring, a small but pretty stone. She has two children from the first husband—two boys, six and four. They live with him in Boston. Her game is the machines. She loves the machines.

"Have you ever hit it big?" I ask.

"I pretty much hit all the time," she says. "Fifty grand here, a hundred grand there. Last year I hit for $350,000. Remember the big one? That was me."

"You're a lucky gambler. You must be loaded."

"Well, no. I mean, I'm not broke—no, but it takes money to make money. I play for the syndicate. You know the doctor?"

"I know the doctor."

"So he gets half and Uncle Sam gets a piece. But still it's fun to win."

"I imagine."

Her beeper goes off. After she checks it, she sighs. "Well, I have to go. It looks like bank number four is about to go, and the doctor wants us to take our places. You know how it is."

I nod.

"You should play for the doctor. Would you like me to ask him?" she says.

"No. I'm independent."

She looks at me. She still has those pretty eyes. "You ever hit?"

"Yeah, lots of times, and I split it with nobody."

She nods her head at this. "Oh. Okay, well, wish me luck."

I raise my Pepsi. "You got it. Luck. Thanks for the 20."

"Thanks for the luck—and the drinks." Laughing, she puts her hand over her mouth.

And like that, she's gone. Good riddance.

She's still a nice girl, but she's falling to pieces. Her tan is gone, her teeth are in disrepair, her clothes are cheap and threadbare—and the way she swallowed those daiquiris, my God, four of them. She's not even a real blonde.

From then on, I would see her in the casinos and avoid her. At most, I would say hi.

Then, about a year later, she walks right up to me and she looks like crap—pale skin, dark rings under her eyes, black teeth. Now she is a platinum fake blonde. And something new. Her smell. I'm not going to talk about her smell. No woman should smell like that. But the worst thing is this horrible boob job. To begin with, they are too big for her rail-thin body, and through her unbuttoned top I can see the red scars where the incisions were made.

She's a bold one these days. She steps right up to my face. "When can I see you?" she asks through blackened and missing teeth. An unlit cigarette dangles from the side of her mouth. It is an ugly mouth. I wish she would hide her mouth with her hand. Has it always been like this? No way. I knew her when. I do the math in my head: E.V. can't be more than 29.

She says again, "When can we get together to talk or whatever?"

I flinch before stammering, "Well, we can have drinks. You can have a daiquiri or two on me."

"Daiquiri?" she says, lighting the cigarette with a lighter that hangs from her neck on a grimy shoelace. "I need something *harder* than a daiquiri."

The way she says it, I'm shocked. This is not E.V. I don't know who this is. I become the adult again. I say, "You're kidding, right?"

"You used to be my bus driver," she says through ugly, cackling laughter. She points to my mouth. "That's the voice you used to use when we were cutting up."

"You guys never cut up. You were good kids."

She starts that unnerving cackle again. Did I make a joke?

"What I really need is some money," she says, wiping her mouth with the back of her hand.

"I don't have any."

But it's hard to keep up with her. Now she's saying, "Can I show you something? I want to show you something. Wait right here, please," and she flashes me those pretty eyes. "Please."

She heads for the ladies' room and ducks inside.

She's gone for like 15 minutes—I'm thinking, This is crazy. What am I waiting here for? I'm thinking about cutting out, but for the good old days, but for the girl she used to be, the girl who used to have those eyes, I wait. Finally, E.V. returns and grabs my hand. "Let's go somewhere so I can show you. Your car."

Well, it has come to this. I have watched E.V. decline. I'm not sure what she is now. Crack addict? Prostitute? I pull my hand away from hers.

"What's this all about?" I say in my sternest voice. "No funny business."

She pleads, "I just want to show you. I promise." She hooks her arm in mine; I smell her body, which is bad enough, but the smoke—no way do I want my wife to smell that.

"And no cigarettes in my car."

E.V. flicks away the cigarette, then clings to me as we walk outside into the early-morning sun.

It is Sunday again. I have been here all night again. My wife's going to chew me out again. Or worse. Thank God I am up a few bucks. Thank God I won tonight. No doubt E.V. has scoped this out. No doubt this is what drew her to me. She saw me win.

We get to my car. I open my door. I am thinking, Her mouth is really ugly—I don't want a blowjob. I don't want to see her ugly breasts. I don't want anything from her. That fake hair. What am I getting myself into?

Against my better judgment, I get in the car and pop the button for E.V., who climbs in on the passenger side, hugging her purse the way hookers do. The early-morning sun is blinding us. We reach up and pull down our sun visors at the same time. E.V. laughs at that. I don't. I'm all business.

"Okay, E.V., what do you want to show me?"

She pulls a slip of paper from her purse. "Read this," she says, passing it to me.

It is written in pencil. It's some kind of poem. I read it out loud:

A Poem for P

There is only one man I love
And it is you
On the weekends when you don't drive me
I am blue

I know my parents may not agree
They'll say you're too old for me
But I love you
I love you my sweet bus driver, P

"What is this, E.V.?"

"You know what it is," she breathes. She pushes the fallen hair back from her face and looks at me with those pretty eyes. "It's a love poem I wrote when I was a kid. I've been carrying it around for 12 years. Sometimes when people are different the world frowns on their love. I was too shy to tell you when I was a kid, but it's all true. I loved you then and I love you now."

"Wow." I am almost touched. Not because of this ugly E.V. in the car with me, but because of who E.V. used to be—not, I repeat, because of who she is now, this desperate, smelly woman too far gone to hide the pencil she wrote this fraudulent note with when she went into the bathroom a few minutes ago. Not because of this woman too far gone to notice, or to care, that she has written the note on the back of an ATM receipt dated today. "Wow," I say for the sake of the E.V. that used to be, "I didn't know you felt that way."

Her eyes are still bluer than this morning's sky. "You can keep it," she says, cuddling close, caressing my face. "I don't need it anymore. I've got you."

I lean away from her smell, pull out my wallet, and pass two hundred-dollar bills into her hand. She kisses me on the neck and exits the car in such a hurry to get back inside the casino that she almost forgets her manners. Almost.

She darts around to my side of the car and says with a little curtsy,

"Goodbye and thank you so much. Thank you, my love."

She blows a kiss.

I watch her backside get smaller as she scurries into the casino. She is wearing a short white skirt. I have watched her becomes this. I have watched E.V. grow up. I have watched E.V. decline.

But from behind, she almost looks like the girl she used to be.

Ah, E.V.

I'm so messed up I swear I don't gamble for like a week.

21.

It is easy to lie to my wife.

She expects everything to be all right, and that is exactly what I tell her. I tell her that everything is all right. It is easier than telling her the truth. Telling her how it really is. If she knew how it really was, I hate to think what she would do. Thank God her nature is to accept rosy, optimistic pictures of ugly truths.

Can she not see what I really am? Can she not see what I am doing to her and our children?

My wife comes from a family of Caribbean elites. In the part of Guyana where she comes from, she has relatives who are judges, lawyers, public officials, and things like that. The part of the country where she comes from is named after her great-great-grandfather, a white man, a British lord, who was once the country's prime minister. Her great-great-grandfather's last name is famous in her country. It is associated with power and money.

Her parents were refugees to America—not the political kind, but they were fleeing the wrath and scorn of her mother's white family. While race-mixing was common and considered for the most part unremarkable during the '60s in Guyana, it set her mother apart in her family, especially since the black man she loved had gotten her with child before wooing, as they say.

So my wife grew up in relative comfort in an affluent Miami suburb with her interracial parents because they had a little money, and they were wise with it. I, on the other hand, grew up in a working-class suburb of Miami called Carol City. I met her because we were bused to the same school during the busing craze of the early '70s.

My wife's mother and father cut a striking figure. He is tall, thick-limbed, and brown as tree bark. Her mom is short, stout, sandy-haired, and freckle-faced. My wife is their second child, the dark-skinned one. Ahead of her, there is an older brother; and after her there are two more boys, a girl, a boy, and then another girl. In all, there are seven children, six of them caramel-colored, one of them dark chocolate. My wife has always had an inferiority complex because of how dark she is compared to her siblings. Maybe that's what made her so different from the rest.

Her brothers and sisters all hold degrees in things like law and medicine. My wife's degree is in political science, though she has never spoken of wanting to go back to school to study law or to become an attorney. She is content to work at the museum in the acquisitions office, where she does not make much money, only a few thousand dollars a year more than me, but is happy doing what she loves and being around what she loves, which is art. Our home, you could say, is a museum. She has an eye for color and arrangement. She has filled our house with pretty things.

I am no fool. I know that in her family, my wife is considered a major disappointment for marrying beneath her station for love rather than to better herself. She is a disappointment because she married a bus driver.

But she likes the rosy picture. She likes to believe. She's got as much faith in me as she has in her church. You should have heard her on the phone with them after I hit that big one. She was putting them in their place. They may have these great careers and whatnot, but how many of them could say that they actually had $100,000 in their bank account? I'm not talking about tied up in investments. I'm talking about hard cash.

She was so convinced that we had finally made it.

Then I had to go and blow it all.

It is easy to make her believe that the money is still there. She has never asked to see the bank statements. I am the man of the house. She is a Caribbean woman. She lets me run things. It is hard to tell her these lies, but it is so easy to make her believe. I am afraid to think what she will do when she finally finds out.

I am so afraid.

I need to win and put that money back.

I don't want to have to steal and pawn my wife's pretty things.

22.

The people at the casinos know me by name.

The people at the CashMyCheck store know me by name.

My bill collectors—I wish they didn't, but they know me by name.

They cut off the water because I had to gamble. They cut off the cable because I had to gamble. They cut off the cell phones because I had to gamble. I had to gamble, I had to gamble, I had to gamble, so I missed taking the boys to see *Spider-Man 2*, which had just come out in the theaters. See, I was on a roll. I had eaten through that big MAX PAY, but I was pretending to my wife that I still had it. The only way to make the bills was to visit the CashMyCheck store twice a month and then delay things as long as I could until I hit a few bucks to pay. Now I really had to gamble. My life and my secret depended on it. Meanwhile, she is shopping and shopping, God bless her, like she's married to a lucky gambler. But I'm the broke kind now.

Today I'm on a roll, and the movie starts at 7:00, but I'm on a roll. I stretch it to 2:00, 3:00, then 4:00, and she finally rings me at 4:30. "Remember the movie?" she says. "Are you gambling?"

"No. I'm here working at the depot getting ready for that field trip tomorrow."

Really, I'm in the bathroom of the casino taking this call so she can't hear the noise of the machines. You know how it is.

I tell her: "I'm leaving the depot right now. I promise."

And the question again is, why *not* leave now? I've made over a grand, which should be good enough for another week of pretending. But right after hanging up the phone, I lose some of it. I am determined to get it all back, so here I am at the table ignoring the ringing cell phone until like 9 p.m.

Yes, I am fully aware that the movie was at 7 and it is now 9. Yes, I am fully aware that I have stood up my boys. Again.

But damnit, I was on a roll.

I get home. She is pissed, cursing and accusing of affairs. Affairs? If not gambling, then it must be affairs. This is how a woman's mind works. The long-suffering wife. It has to be another woman. Affairs, affairs, affairs. Yes, yes, yes. My other woman is the casino, hon.

I swear, sometimes I wish I were having an affair with a woman who would take a couple hundred bucks a month to love me up and leave the rest of my goddamned money alone. Pussy means nothing to me. I wish I did love pussy like I used to. Gambling is fun. That's what people don't understand about gamblers. We gamble to gamble. We play to play. We don't play to win. If we did, I would have given up after I hit more than triple my annual income instead of giving all of it back in less than six months.

It is July. See, when I hit that big wad last October I was thinking, Man oh man, I have enough money here to keep everybody happy and to go gamble, too. I was thinking, Man, I am set for life. I can take care of things at home and go gamble, too. See? It's always about the gamble. Everything else is secondary. Okay, I miss *Spider-Man 2*. So I get cursed out by my wife as usual and go to bed high on the grand I won tonight. It is one-one-hundredth of what I need to get back on top. If I'm lucky like this for 100 more days, I'll be back on top in three months. The next day when I get home from work, my wife informs me that my neighbor has taken the boys to see *Spider-Man 2* with his family. The neighbor is a good man, a family man, who does not gamble.

"But I wanted to take them."

She doesn't even dignify my statement with a response. We both know I'm lying. Somewhere deep inside I am still that good father who wanted to take his sons to see *Spider-Man 2*.

It's too sad. I can't focus on it. When I focus on sadness, I get an overwhelming urge to gamble.

So now I am sad. So now I have the urge. Since the boys are at the movies anyway, I am free. I am off the hook. I take a quick shower, then hop in the car and go gamble.

I have a bad night.

I give back $800 from last night's winnings.

When I come home and check that night's Cash-3, my area code has played.

3-0-5.

And the Play-4? The last four digits of my cell phone.

1-1-7-7.

Now even God is playing mind games with me.

Or maybe He's trying to tell me something.

Tell me something I don't know, Lord. Tell me the numbers before they hit, not after.

23.

My first child was a beautiful little girl I had by this other woman I dated before I married my wife and had the three boys.

Four, it used to be, but one of them is dead.

So this woman, who had grown to be a pain in the butt, finally moved herself and my daughter up to Maryland a few years ago, which is okay because she is less of a pain in the butt when she is far away, but here's the thing: I am a good father and I love my daughter, who is enrolled up there in junior college now. So tell me this, why is it that when my ex called and said they were falling on hard times up there and could I send her a few hundred, I said okay, then went out and gambled away half of my paycheck, then went to the CashMyCheck store for this high interest (10 percent), short-term (two weeks) loan to pay the rest of my bills, then ignored the bills and my constantly ringing cell phone, too, because I couldn't believe that my daughter and her mother could be getting kicked out of their house up there, and instead of helping out, I was blowing what little extra I had?

I could get kicked out of my house, too.

Foreclosure and divorce loom.

The IRS is no fun.

I wish I had that hundred grand back.

Make me lucky again, Lord, so that I may be great again in my daughter's eyes.

24.

I have like three grand left from a jackpot of $100,000.

Then I discover this new machine, the diamond game.

It's just like the regular machine, except it sends you these diamonds every once in a while that are wild cards. It doesn't pay big, but it pays often. I hit a little jackpot right off for $5,000. So now I'm back up to eight grand. Thank God. I can survive on that if I stop gambling.

Yup.

Then I hit another little one for $2,300. Thank God. Then I hit a couple really small ones for $800, $700, $1,100, like that on this generous machine. I'm doing okay again. Close to 13 grand in the bank. Only $87,000 more to go and I'll be back on top. We take a trip to the Keys. The whole family. I resist the urge to get on the gambling boat. We fish all day and night. My boys are great company. I can't believe how they've grown. They are so funny. They make me laugh. The one who used to be allergic to strawberries and dust and pet hair has outgrown it completely and now he's always befriending stray dogs and cats, and strawberries are his favorite fruit (though it still worries us). The quiet one has a girlfriend that the other two keep teasing him about. The oldest one has snuck and pierced his ear, and I'm trying to decide how I feel about it—his mother hates it, but I think it makes him look fierce, and I think maybe the girls go for that these days. Maybe . . . maybe I can do it. Maybe I can make it.

I get back up to Miami. I don't go to the casinos for three weeks. I actually deposit two consecutive paychecks without going to the casinos. It is good not smelling like smoke. It is good not lying to my wife. It is good being home early. It is good helping my children with their homework. It is good making love. I make love to my wife two nights in a row. I make love to her three times in one night. I fly up to Maryland to see my daughter. I give her mother two grand.

She tells me in private: "They were going to take our house. We were living off her scholarship money. I prayed that something would happen. I prayed to God, and God always delivers. I didn't think it would come from you because I know like you told me you are having financial problems. But God is a miracle worker. This money is blessed money. This is exactly how much I prayed for. I can give $800 to the mortgage. I can use another $500 to pay the rest of the bills. I still have $700 left over to add to my paycheck and your child support, which just came in the mail from the state."

Then she kisses me, which creeps me out. My dislike of her is tremendous. We don't get along at all. But it's okay. I understand how she feels. But what I find amazing is that she thinks $2,000 is a lot of money.

Two grand?

I can blow that in two hours in a casino.

I do blow that in two hours in a casino.

Then I fly back down to Miami and have five bad days. I lose $1,100, $1,100, $700, $800, $1,100. I am in shock. Where has the luck gone? It's that damned woman. I shouldn't have let her kiss me. She's bad luck. She stole my daughter from me and now she's given me bad luck. Look at all this money I have lost. I am right back where I was. Worse. Because now I really want to gamble. I don't want to do anything else but gamble. I'm not going to let anything stand in my way. I will call in sick to work. I will lie to my wife, whom I love. I will take money from the children's accounts. I will sell the junk I have in the garage. I will borrow from two CashMyCheck stores. I will borrow from friends. I will borrow from strangers. I will steal from my wife. I will have money to gamble.

I will win it all back.

25.

I am losing with pocket aces.

I am losing with Big Slick.

The machines are laughing at me. The machines are sucking money like reverse ATMs. I have never been in a slump like this. Get that camera off my back, you damned Indians. Play fair.

I meet this woman, C.L., outside the casino one Saturday afternoon. I am beating a hasty retreat to my car. As usual. I am muttering loudly that I have just blown $2,000. Again. She passes me, this stringy-haired, skinny white woman, and says, "I know what you mean."

I tell her, "This is never going to happen again."

She says, looking straight at me, "Oh yes it will."

With the intimacy of kindred strangers, we start comparing notes. She is sneaking money from the man she loves.

She says, "The sad thing is that he trusts *me* with his money. If he only knew. I have to borrow from my mother to cover all his money I'm losing here at the casino. The way I figure it, though, once I hit it big, I'll pay him back and tell him all about it. It'll be like I invested his money for him."

"I know what you mean," I say. "My wife thinks we're well off because I hit last year. She doesn't know that I pretty much blew in seven months maybe $100,000, and then some. Of course, it's more than that.

Where the hell is my salary? I do have a job. I do receive a paycheck every two weeks. That's gone, too."

"Tell me about it. I hit for 20 grand last year. Where is it?"

"How would I know? I'm still looking for my hundred."

"I'll tell you where it is—it's in there," she says, pointing at the casino entrance.

"In there. Yes."

"When I hit, I paid a few bills, I gave my mom some expensive gifts. Then I came back here and pretty much blew the rest."

"It goes fast."

"Doesn't it, though?"

"We tip big when we win."

"I was passing out hundreds like dimes."

"I bought a new car."

"That's what I should have done. At least you bought a car. I hit for 20 grand and I'm driving a car falling apart."

"I can't put gas in mine."

She shrugs. "Well, there you have it."

I say, "We live to gamble."

"Gambling is fun."

"Lots of fun. Look at the fun we're having."

"I'm supposed to be at work right now, but I called in sick so I could gamble."

"I'm supposed to be in— Check this out, I got you beat. I'm supposed to be in a meeting right now that will determine whether I keep my job or not."

"What do you do?"

"Well, one of my jobs, my main job, is a school bus driver."

"That's a good job. Good benefits."

"And I drive a tour bus on the weekends."

"Okay."

"And I work at the Turkey Point Nuclear Power Plant at night. Security. That's where I'm supposed to be right now. They're having this mandatory training session for terrorism."

"But you're here."

"Having fun."

C.L. understands everything without being told. She knows why I work three jobs: in order to fund my gambling. She knows why I am missing the meeting: How dare they schedule a mandatory meeting during my gambling time? She knows why I am relatively untroubled about missing the mandatory meeting: The longer you do a thing, the better you become at it. Not gambling, but lying to support your gambling. She knows that as a gambler, I am so good at lying that any mandatory meeting I miss will be forgiven because of one of my expert lies: My Mother had kidney failure (which is true, but last week, not this week), I am so distraught over it (over money), I had to rush her to the hospital (last week); in fact, I'm calling you from the hospital (from the bathroom of the casino so that you cannot hear the singing of the machines); I'm sorry I missed the mandatory meeting, it won't happen again (yes it will, yes it will, yes it will, probably tomorrow).

"So many jobs," she says, "and you're still broke."

"Is that crazy or what?"

"You're a gambler."

"Yup, yup, yup. But all I need to do is hit it big one more time."

"We've got money for nothing but gambling."

"And time for nothing but finding money to gamble."

"Tell me something I don't know," C.L. says.

"I almost hit the Play-4 for 40 grand on Super Bowl Sunday."

"No! You mean the night that 7-7-9-9 played?"

I love this woman!

"Yup, yup, yup." I flip open my wallet and show her my eight Super Bowl very close losers.

"Amazing," she says, showing the appropriate reverence as she carefully inspects each ticket. "If you had hit this, it would have gotten you back on your feet."

"Yes, and I didn't box it. Not one single time."

"You are so brave," she says with something like admiration. "You go all the way. You don't hold back."

"No, I don't."

She's looking at me with admiration. C.L. Hmmm.

Then we exchange phone numbers and vow to support each other. This is not a sex thing, though she is cute in a skinny-white-girl sort of way. The dirty-blond hair. The green eyes. The butchy, braless, perky-breasted T-shirt look. The ATM receipts bulging the pockets of her jeans. This is not lust. We are gamblers.

Gamblers, I think, are another sexual persuasion altogether. We are attracted only to poker tables and slot machines. Not necessarily to each other.

But C.L., she understands me. She really does.

I would do her.

26.

I get brave and count my ATM receipts.

They are hidden everywhere. In the car: in the glove compartment, in the ashtray, under the seats, under the floor mats, under the CD tray, under the CDs, in the empty CD cases, in the empty CD sleeves, in the toolbox under the coil of jumper cables, in every sleeve of every sun visor, in the auto wallet with the manual, proof of insurance, and registration. In the house: in the pockets of pants I no longer wear, under the bed, in seldom-worn shoes, in socks, in my bureau drawers, in shirt pockets, in my Father's Day jewel box (the expensive rings, cuff links, and watches having already been pawned), in every folder in every drawer in the filing cabinet I bought to keep important household documents like insurance policies, the children's birth certificates, immunization records, and report cards. It takes half a day to gather them all. They fill most of three lawn bags. There are more in my locker at the depot and on my bus and at my mother's house and my big sister's and in my wallet (at least 10 from yesterday). And still there must be more. Where are last year's? The year before? I take out my calculator, stick a pencil behind my ear, and clear a space on the kitchen table. I am going to do this thing. I am going to do this. The wife and kids are not due back from the church picnic until late. But it is hard. I am not halfway through one bag, and I am already up to $47,000. How can that be? I am a bus driver. I withdrew $47,000 to gamble?

That's . . . impossible.

And the fees?

At an average of $2.00 per withdrawal (since each casino ATM charges a different fee), and I'm looking at about 500 or so receipts—good God—that's $1,000 in ATM fees alone. And I am only halfway through one bag. I snatch the pencil from behind my ear and fling it against the wall. I bury my head in my hands. I can't do it. I can't do it. I can't do it. Can you imagine me sitting down with these bags and an accountant?

Is it any wonder I don't do my taxes?

I take my three lawn bags out to the toolshed and hide them in the back, behind the unused stacked-up ceramic tiles from when we did the floors.

My family won't be back until late, but today, for the first time in a long while, I have no urge to go gambling.

I have no urge to do anything but sit on the floor of my toolshed and think.

I can always go back to the community college. In two or three years I can have a degree. In two or three years I can have— Do I have two or three years? Do I even have two or three months? The IRS . . .

My thoughts turn dark.

I am not lucky. I am just not lucky, that's all.

I sit for another hour on the floor of my shed.

Then I go out and buy a gun.

27.

There's a new kid, Russian—been here only a couple months, but he speaks the language pretty good. Better than some of the natives. He sits up front with the junior high smarties while the rowdies are cutting up in the back. I hear the honors girl asking him about his life back in his country, his family, how many brothers and sisters, his school, was it named after Stalin or Lenin. The Russian kid says, "9-9-8," and I look up in the mirror at him. He's thin with very pink skin. He's got shoulders that jut out and long, thin arms. The baseball cap he wears sits too big on his elfish, dirty-blond head.

"9-9-8?" I ask as I stop at a light.

The kid says, "Yes, where I come from in Russia, the schools have numbers not names."

"So you are Mr. 9-9-8?" I say. "Hello, Mr. 9-9-8."

Some of the fools in the back hear that and turn their cackling attention to him. The Russian kid pulls his cap down over his eyes and mumbles his real name. Boris. The other students get a good laugh out of that, too. Boris Bad-e-nuff, they joke. Boris the Russian. Boris Boris Rhymes with Doris, Tie Him Up and Dump Him in the Forest. Boris the faggot. Boris, is you a Russian spy? Somebody betta call 007 for Boris ass. Boris, embarrassed, is lost under that cap, his bony shoulders folded in like wings. I shout to the others to shut up, cut it out, or they'll be written up. That quiets them a bit, gets them off his back. I say to Boris the Russian kid, "Don't you worry about those fools back there. You just tell your folks to play 9-9-8 in the Cash-3 tonight."

Why did I tell him that? He's just a kid. Why would I want to get him started down that path? What the hell is wrong with me? This is crossing the line.

But it is a sign.

That night and for the next three nights, I play 9-9-8 in the Cash-3—five and then 10 dollars worth of tickets. I need to hit and I need to hit big. Finally, on Sunday night I give up and go back to playing my contract 2-3-2. Of course, that is the night 9-9-8 comes in straight, and I am sitting there with this stupid 2-3-2 which hasn't hit in like three years. If I had just played 9-9-8 one more night it would have paid $500. I sure could have used it. Damn. Damn.

The next day is Monday and I'm behind the wheel again. I'm trying to be chill, I'm trying to be calm, though I am on edge. The rowdies are cutting up in the back as usual and Boris is saying something to the honors-student black girl, who has now become his friend. I think she's got a crush on him. I know she's got a crush on me. She sometimes brings me food. She sometimes lends me money. Boris tells her, "My father spent a lot of money on it. I think he won like $5,000 or something

like that. He was very happy. He was very grateful to the bus driver."
His blue-gray eyes catch mine in the mirror and he smiles. "How much
money did you win on 9-9-8, Mr. Bus Driver?"

"Not one damn penny," I say too sharply to Mr. 9-9-8's eyes. These
damn numbers. This damn addiction. I need to win. I need it. I need it
like I need air.

As I get back to my driving, some of the rowdies, who heard me
say "damn," are echoing it and cracking derivative jokes: "Damn penny,"
"Damn Russian," "Damn bus driver," "Damn school bus," "Damn
school."

When we get to the school, I hold my honors girl back while the
others get off. I chitchat with her good-naturedly, then get down to telling her how much I need. She opens her cute little purse, all flirtatious
and ladylike, and gives me all she's got, a five and four singles. I put it in
my pocket and utter grand promises of paying her back double tomorrow. She points to the bulge in my coat and says, "What's that?"

I pass my hand over the bulge, thinking maybe it's a wad of ATM
receipts. It's the gun. I have brought the gun on the junior high school
bus.

Twenty-five minutes later I am at the casino, where I blow every
penny of my honors girl's nine dollars. I have crossed the line.

I have crossed way over the line.

My Name Is P

28.

I'm going through my things. I find my New Year's resolution from four years ago. *Stay away from G* is at the top of the list. I wrote it in code in case my wife found it. That is followed by *Pay more attention to your children*. My son was becoming a delinquent when I wrote that. He became one, or he already was one. He joined a gang, or maybe he was already in it. He shot a kid. Then another kid shot him. It was a gang thing. It was in the papers. You might have read about it. This dead son was our first child together, my wife's and mine. We took it hard, considering all of our problems. We would have divorced, probably, if we didn't have the three other boys. My son's death came almost a year to the day after I won that first royal, and I think that that had something to do with it. He was always a very private child. Independent. Secretive. Maybe I wasn't paying enough attention to him. Maybe that's an easy answer. Something I heard on *Oprah*. I know you don't want to hear this, and I'm ashamed to say it, but I feel I have to. I really loved my son. His death hit me hard. I stopped gambling for an entire month after he died. I wish I had been there for him more. He was a beautiful boy. Tall and raw-boned, with a handsome dark face and cheekbones so sharp that when he smiled his eyes disappeared into slits. The thing I'm ashamed to tell you is that he was named after me, he was a Junior, and he was born on the exact same day I was born on, but 23 years later. You see where this is going? The day he was born on, 23 years after me, was the 23rd. I know that this is sick, but it's the truth. You know how we are. We see patterns. I was playing that 2-3-2-3-2-3 in memory of my son. My sweet little Junior. I never told my wife what number I was playing when I won. She might have taken it the wrong way. She would have killed me. At any rate, she used some of that money to change his cheap headstone to a real nice one. I made a vow to visit that head-stone once a month on the 23rd. I haven't visited it once since he died. On the 23rd, like most days, I'm at a casino gambling. Yesterday was the 23rd. I was at the casino against my vow, against the court order. I blew $800 on the 23rd . . . Am I the sickest person here? Am I the sickest one here or what? Am I the sickest one here? Am I the sickest?

I'm shouting it over and over to the room. *Am I the sickest one here?*

I want to cry out. I want to shed big tears.

I want to gamble.

The rest of them in the room are nodding their heads like, Yeah, we know, we've been there, we've been there, we've been there, and we don't ever want to go back, but not a day goes by that we don't feel the pull. Some of them are taking note of the 2-3 to play it tonight in the Cash-3 or Play-4, or maybe that's me talking, because 2-3 hasn't hit in such a long time it's due to hit soon.

Am I the sickest one here?

"My name is P, I am a gambler, and I am the sickest one here."

O.C. puts a hand on my shoulder as I fall apart. I am crying real tears. "Baby steps," O.C. says, "baby steps. Take them one at a time. Take it one day at a time. One day at a time, P. You can do it."

I hear myself say, "I got the other boys, I got my daughter. She's this very smart young lady who looks up to me. She wanted to be a school bus driver just like me when she was a kid. It was so cute. I used to take her everywhere with me. She's a smart girl, now she wants to be a doctor. I need to send her money. I need to help out more. Pleeease . . ."

"Baby steps. Baby steps."

". . . help me, pleeease . . . It's just . . . it's just . . . I hate . . ."

"One day at a time."

" . . . I hate this place . . . Don't be mad at me, O.C., don't be mad . . ."

"One day at a time."

". . . I could be gambling right now . . . that's where I want to be . . . I hate being here because I'm not there . . . I want to be there . . ."

"It's okay, P. We've all been there."

". . . Make me hate it, make me hate it, or when I leave here, I'm going straight there."

"Your children. Think about your children."

"I love them. But when I am with them, I want to be . . . at the casino."

"One day at a time, P."

". . . There is where I always want to be. I want to be nowhere else."

"You will lose it all, P. Is that what you want? You want to lose everything?"

"There is always the chance that I will win."

"You will just lose it all back. You'll lose more."

"Not if I win big . . . not talking about no damn hundred thousand. If I win a million, that will be enough. That will take care of all my problems."

"If you win a million, they will still take it back. The amount doesn't matter when you're throwing it to the wind. The amount doesn't matter when you're setting it on fire. Remember what E.F. said? E.F. won a million and lost it back, plus three more million."

E.F. is nodding his head in pathetic agreement. My tears are gone. The smug bastard is really pissing me off. "No offense, E.F., but you are weak. I would never lose a million dollars. It's too much. You have to be sick to lose a million dollars." Then I shrug off O.C.'s hand. "Don't compare me to E.F. anymore, O.C., okay? E.F. is sick. With the kind of money his family has, he had to be sick to be gambling in the first place. He needs a place like this. I don't."

"P—"

"I hate this place."

"P—"

"I hate this place!"

"P, we're trying to save your life."

I yell, "God help me, God help me, God help me! It's hopeless. I want to die. I want to die. If I can't gamble, I want to die. I don't sleep at night anymore. I want to die. I can't explain it. I can't explain it . . . I want to die."

"Me too!" O.C. says suddenly. "I want to die. I want to die. I want to die."

Then he punches me in the chest. The shock of it is stronger than the actual physical impact. I wasn't expecting to be punched.

He says, "I had a daughter who loved me. I had a wife. I had a house. I had a career. I had a daily gambling habit of 10 grand. I used to be a millionaire. You used to know me probably. I used to be a professional football player. I was great in college. I was good enough for the pros—at least for the year I lasted before it finally caught up with me. I played for these same Miami Dolphins right down here. I backed up Marino that one year, remember? No? What does it matter? I blew through two million dollars in six months. I blew myself out of the National Football League, P, because I like to play slot machines more than football. Isn't that funny, P? How throwing a football on national TV pales in comparison to pushing the *PLAY* button on a slot machine? How being famous looks like nothing next to a deck of cards and a smoke-filled room? How cashing a paycheck every week that has five zeros on it doesn't even come close to looking into your hand and finding a pair of aces in the hole? How a blackjack table was more beautiful than my wife, and she was a Miss Texas? Wife? Wife? The casino was my wife. This makes sense? This makes sense?"

O.C. is punching my chest each time he asks a question. Yeah, I remember him from the Dolphins' bench. The All-American good looks. The rangy height. The big hands. I'm not a sports bettor but I would have bet on him to take them to the Super Bowl. He is still punching me. It hurts. It hurts, but not the punches.

He says, "This makes sense? This makes sense? I can only explain this to another gambler. I can only explain this to you. I want to die. Every day I don't gamble, I want to die. I haven't gambled in seven years, and I want to die. I can only explain this to you, P. I can only explain this to a gambler like you. I'm glad I met you, P. Thank you for saving my life today. I was going to kill myself again today, but meeting you saved my life. I have never met a sicker degenerate than you, P. Thanks for saving me. Thanks a lot, and you better thank me back. You may not love us, but we're all that stands between you and the darkness, buddy. And see you again tomorrow night, or I'm calling the court, I swear to God. My name is O.C. and I am a gambler. Good night, fuckhead, whether you sleep or not."

O.C.'s walking out the door. I can't believe it. I wait until he's completely gone before I say to the others: "Can you believe that guy? What an ass. He's so full of himself. Who does he think he is?"

But they're walking out the door, too. No one takes me on.

29.

I am full of air now wherever I am.

At home, that is where I feel it the most. My wife and I are not together since court. The IRS had no right to arrest her, too, but everything we owned was joint. I tried to explain to them that it was all my doing, that she had no idea what was going on, but they did not care. So we got a quickie divorce. She is suing me, but not for real. Just on paper. It is only to protect her assets, her art things and the things her parents gave her. I am okay with that. If I go down, I want to go down alone. Now our accounts are separate. I don't have access to the direct deposit from her job anymore. It used to come in handy. Sometimes I would steal a few dollars from it when things were being turned off, sneak over to the casino, turn that into enough to get things turned back on, then sneak the money back into her account so she could continue the dream about the good life she was having with me. Sometimes she would say, Why did they turn off the water? And I would answer, Yeah. That. I went down there and had to cuss them out. There was a mix-up in their computer again. She was so trusting. She never asked to see the bank statements. Now she knows what was really going on. Those days are over now, and the lies, too. We still sleep in the same bedroom, but not in the same bed. I am on the floor. In front of the boys, we are still husband and wife, Mommy and Daddy. The boys are at funny ages: 15, 14, and 11. Neither of us wants another dead son. We have agreed it's good to have me around just for show. I sleep on the floor. There is no sex.

This is your punishment, she says. You did this to yourself.

These days she has taken to wearing sexy underwear to bed. She wants me to want her. This is supposed to be torture. If I wanted her, this would be torture—seeing her like that. What she doesn't understand is that to me sex is . . . well, if she came right out and told me to take it, I guess I would have to, but making love to her is not something I'm really interested in doing. She is not my type anymore.

She doesn't gamble.

30.

I am learning to tell time outside a casino's walls—time with clocks and natural light, time not measured in antes and flops, and trips to the ATM, and grinning, winning Chinese—a different kind of time than what I'm used to. It seems like weeks when only a day has passed if I am not gambling. How can I make it to the next day? Everything is dull to me. I am distracted. I am only half here. I am full of air it feels like. Something used to be in there, but now it is gone.

The days seem to drag on and drag on.

I am at home, I am at work, and it is all the same to me. At work, the children get rowdy on the bus, but that is not real to me. At work, they have found out about my permanent part-time jobs, which is both not against county policy and against it at the same time. Yes, we can do it, but we have to have it approved by our supervisor, who will say yes or no based upon our most recent evaluations. My supervisor tells me the new rules: No more moonlighting—if you don't like it, you can hit the road.

He has never liked me. His words are air. Before I got demoted back to bus driver five years ago, I used to be his supervisor. Why was I demoted?

Too many days off.

Why so many days off?

Let's see, it was the year the Rams won the Super Bowl.

It was a very good year.

31.

All the time I am assessing and devising.

Where did I go wrong?

I had lacked discipline. I would be winning at poker, then lose focus and start giving it back. I would be banging a losing machine, and then double or triple my bet and lose more. How illogical. At my worst, I would play two or three machines at the same time. Losing even more money. And even on those days—almost every one of those losing days, at some point in the losing, I would start to win again. True, I wouldn't always get all of my money back, but I would get a good portion of it, only to lose it again. Now my memory is crystal. I remember being down $800, then hitting $500. A little resurgence money. But instead of walking away down $300, I would give it all back. If I could get back even half of that resurgence money they gave me, I would be a very wealthy man right now. I remember being down a grand and getting back $1,100. I am up $100 after losing! But I would give it all back. Can you believe it? Can you believe how crazy I was?

In the old days before I was a gambler, I would go into a casino and hit $20 and walk out screaming *Hallelujah!* I remember hitting $100 before I was a gambler and running straight to the bank to deposit it. These days $100 is nothing to me. What am I going to do with that? A hundred? You might as well put three pennies in my hand.

My poor mother.

She says, "I will give you an allowance every month from your father's pension. He would have wanted you to have it."

"Mom, you don't have enough for yourself."

"I will give it and you will take it."

"Mom, but you need it."

"Take the money. I am old and you are young. The only reason you started gambling in the first place is that times were hard and bosses weren't paying people what they should have. You had no other choice. You were trying to do well by your family. I'm not ashamed of you at all. I hate the IRS."

"Mom."

"Take the money. Take it."

And I do.

It's $15—.

Ah, Mom.

Both her kidneys have failed. She is on dialysis. There are other complications. My mother will be following my father soon.

But I take the money.

32.

When my mother dies, I am nearly inconsolable.

There is only one cure.

The only way out of this is to go on a gambling binge.

But I am barred.

Oh my God, no. Mama. Oh, Mama. What am I going to do without you?

Mama! Mama! Mommy!

33.

C.L. calls me once in a while, and we talk in whispers over our cell phones, kinda like an affair, though we don't really have to do that because I am not really married anymore. C.L. says, "Are you being strong?"

"I'm trying. Are you?"

"It's hard."

"It *is* hard."

"My man found out."

"Mmm. How did he take it?"

"He got . . . rough."

"No!"

"I had no choice but to take it."

"No, no."

"I had to let him do it, or lose him," she says. "He found out that I had eaten through his life's savings. I was in charge of it. He trusted me unconditionally—I ate right through it. The look on his face when he found out how little was left. He kept saying, You *gambled* it away? He couldn't grasp the concept. *Gambled?* He kept saying it, like maybe he wanted me to say I had given it to a man. He would have been happier if I had said that. *Gambled?* he said over and over. He's never been to a casino in his life."

"They don't understand us. Damnit, nobody understands us. But are you okay now?"

"You mean physically or gamblically?"

I laugh. She laughs.

"He's a softy. I had the black eye for a few weeks. No lovey-dovey for a few months. He even moved out for a while, but he's back now.

Things are still tense," she says. "As far as gambling is concerned, I've had better weeks. This week has been bad. That damn diamond machine. A Chinese man hit a jackpot right next to me two times in three hours, can you believe it? They always pay the Chinese. I wish I was Chinese. But to me it's paying nothing. Nothing." She sighs for both of us. Yeah. I know what she means. She says, "You want to get together for a bit?"

"I didn't tell you I'm barred from the casinos?"

"Oh no."

"Oh yeah. Uncle Sam don't play."

"Oh no, no. You poor thing," she says. There is a peacefulness now as we hold the phones to our ears without speaking. We take comfort in the sound of each other's breathing. It's almost like love, this honesty, but without the sadness or the guilt. There is another one out there. There is another one out there like me. She says tenderly, "You still carrying those Super Bowl losers around in your pocket?"

"You know it."

"Very, very close losers," she says. "I'd like to see them again."

"I'd like to show them to you again."

"I'd like to see more than those tickets."

"I'd like to show you more than those tickets."

Her voice brightens. "Are you flirting with me, P?"

"Are you flirting with me, C.L.?"

"Yes, I am. Yes, indeedy, I am."

"I am too, C.L. I'm flirting with you."

"But do you mean it?"

"Do *you*?"

"To tell you the truth," she says, "I like you just fine, but I'd rather have a good day at the casino."

"I know where you're coming from. There's nothing I would like more than to see you naked, except of course to play the 7s and 3s I've been dreaming about on that diamond machine."

She had been my pusher. And I hers. This was during the couple of times we got together at the casino. When she hit a decent bump on the machines and it looked like she was losing it back, I would push her off the seat and print her ticket before she could lose it all. Sometimes I would grab her purse and exit the casino with it before she could reach for her ATM card again. She did the same for me, pushing me off the seat or grabbing my wallet. We watched each other's backs. We were a team, but now all that was over.

"Barred for life," she says. "Ow. That must really suck, P."

"Yes, it does."

"Then I guess that means you're never going to see me naked," she says.

34.

There is not one waking moment when I am not devising.

If I can't work part-time, I reason, then there is no way to pay the bills and pay the IRS, except by gambling.

It has been three months, and I have been going back in disguise for about two weeks. The wide-brimmed hat, the dark shades.

Caution has made me a better gambler. I don't stay too long. I never try for the big jackpots anymore, the ones over $1,199, because then it has to be reported to Uncle Sam. I never use anything associated with my bank—no ATMs, no credit cards, no checks. My bank is being monitored. It is strictly cash these days. But no one monitors the cash in the seats of a school bus, so at least I have that to fall back on.

Also, my extended family now knows about my situation, and they have shown surprising compassion. I wonder if it has anything to do with the unselfish bounty I used to share with them when I was lucky. Secretly, they want me to win like that again. I am always good for $20 here and there from the cuzzes and the aunties. It always, always, always comes with a lecture, but then I am on my way in my hat and shades to the side doors of the casino. I play the cheapo poker tables, 50 cents mostly, and sometimes the dollar game. I am on a roll. I have won every time I have been there these past two weeks. Sometimes when I leave, I have over $60 in my wallet. I am multiplying my initial investment by three. I am earning close to $40 a day, which works out to $1,200 a month. I am earning $40 in about an hour, which is how long I allow myself to sit at the table. When I am done, I get up and sprint past the machines, which still beckon.

I go home and put the money in a shoebox under the bed. I help the boys with their homework. I watch the insipid program or two on TV until I hear my ex-wife snoring in her pretty underwear. I count the money in the box in the dark. It is $600 now. I am laden with regret. If I had been this disciplined back when I was starting out, I could have made $100,000 without ever having to hit it big on a machine.

These are my new rules: Take only a small amount of money into the casino with you. Do not carry ATM cards, credit cards, or a checkbook. Don't make friends with luck. Make friends with God. God is real. God is on your side. If you are losing, say Thank you, Lord, I will live to gamble another day, and take what's left of your money off the table. There is no shame in losing. Learn to be a good loser. Lose with a smile and a prayer. Always leave with money, even if it is a quarter. Set a time limit. Abide by the limit you have set. When it is time to leave, leave quickly. When it is time to leave, run. Run fast. Finally, do not fall in love with the casino. The casino is a selfish, stingy, jealous bitch. The casino is the most beautiful bitch in the world.

At any rate, I am on a two-week roll. I'm going to try to make it last forever. Tomorrow night I will go to GA. I will take my blows from O.C. It's okay. He means well. I will focus on my dead mother and son to ease the pain. How happy they made me. How much I loved them. How badly I let them down.

When GA is over, I will sneak up to the casino, and I will earn another $40 or leave with at least a dollar in my pocket.

Now that the issue is settled in my mind, I push my shoebox full of cash and the loaded gun (for just in case) back under my ex-wife's bed. I stretch out on the bedding she has spread on the floor for me.

I do not feel like crying tonight over my mother's cheap, shitty-ass funeral.

I do not feel like suicide tonight.

I feel like I'm holding aces.

I feel . . . sexual excitement. I am surprised to find myself excited.

Now what do I do with this? How do I cash this in?

I sit up and peep at my ex-wife's prone body above the covers, her beautiful body bathed in the moonlight streaming in from outside. On that bed in this room in this house that we may yet lose, she is snoring peacefully. Good for her. Good for her. It is good that she can sleep. I can't. I still can't, not on a mere one hour of gambling per day. Not when there's all that free money in the casino and I can't even take a shot at it. But she looks good, and she can sleep.

Let her sleep.

My excitement is gone. It was all an illusion. I have no pocket aces. No Big Slick. I lay myself down on the bedding on the floor. My eyes are wide open. They will remain open most of the night, as they do every night. They will see visions. They will see numbers.

I can't believe I did this to myself.

I shake my head from side to side.

I can't believe I did this.

I Must Make Amends

35.

(A Second Definition of Insanity)

I can't sleep.

I want that shoebox.

36.

I see my dead mother. I see my dead son. I see numbers. I see my dead mother and son and numbers. These are their Social Security numbers and the numbers on the fraudulent credit cards I made in their names so that I could have money to gamble. I can't sleep. I am a degenerate. I am shit. I am shit.

I want to die.

37.

There's a fairy tale they tell sometimes.

Once upon a time, there was this son of a gambler who decided that he would not become a gambler because he saw how gambling had destroyed his father's life. So he refused to become addicted to the casino. He would spend only a dollar a day in the casino and then leave right away, and thus he came to be called Dollar Danny.

So Dollar Danny went to the casino every day and put his dollar in the machine. Usually it lost, and he would leave right away. Sometimes it won—small stuff, $20, $30, $50—and still he would cash out after that one single push and leave right away. They should have called him One-Push Danny, the way he played. He had such discipline.

So this went on for like 20 years, until one day when Dollar Danny pushed his push and the machine began to sing the jackpot song. *Ping-ping! Ping-ping-ping!* He had won $20,000!

Everybody began to slap Dollar Danny on the back. Some of them joked, Now you will surely become a degenerate like us. That's all it takes is one big win and then you're sucked in. You'll see. You'll spend that 20 grand so fast it'll be like you never won it at all. Ha-ha. We'll give you a year, Danny. One year. You'll see.

But the next day, they all watched in awe as Dollar Danny came into the casino, put his dollar in, pushed the machine one single time, and then walked out.

He did it just like that—one dollar a day—for the next 20 years, until he won 20 grand again.

And that's the end of the tale.

The way it was explained to me, Dollar Danny had a secret that none of the other gamblers knew about. They never asked where he went after he had pushed his single push. Where did he go? He went straight to the bank and deposited one single dollar. He put one dollar in the bank in an interest-bearing account for every dollar he put in the machine. Of course, whenever he hit the small stuff, he put that in the bank, too. So before he had hit his first jackpot, Dollar Danny had banked well over 20 grand in single dollars and "small stuff," and it had grown, with interest, to well over $35,000.

Dollar Danny's secret that the other gamblers did not know was that when he hit that $20,000 the first time, to him it was just more "small stuff."

I never did like that fairy tale. I never did understand it.

I still don't.

In my book, Dollar Danny is a pussy.

O.C. told me this story.

O.C. is a pussy. I hate GA. GA is like a religion. GA is like a really stifling religion. There are too many steps to climb. I can't climb 12 steps. Why can't there be a one-step program? Why can't there be a no-step program? That's the program for me. No steps. Just snap your fingers and you're normal again.

But life is no fairy tale.

You've got to be in it to win it.

I want my shoebox.

38.

(A Third Definition of Insanity)

". . . Insanity is defined as doing the same thing over and over and expecting a different result."

"Shut up, O.C. I know that one already."

"It's the truth, P."

"Shut up, O.C.! Leave me alone! Why don't you all just leave me alone? I'm losing my mind. I need to gamble! I need to gamble! Don't you understand? It's my life!"

"What about your wife and children?"

"Fuck them!"

"P!"

"I'm dying. I'm dying like this. I need it so bad. I'm dying."

". . . P, poor P."

"I miss my mom, I miss her so much. Oh, Mama, what did I do? I'm dying, can't you see?"

39.

(It's My Shoebox, and I Want It)

I can't sleep. I can't sleep.

Mama, Junior, I'm sorry. I'm sorry. I'm sorry. Leave me alone. I want my shoebox. I loved you, but I love this more. I'm just so weak. When I get rich I'll make it all up to you. I'll make it up to everybody.

I can't live like this. I can't live like this. There is a beautiful, half-naked ex-wife in bed just waiting for me to shape up so that she can give me one more chance, and I do not want to shape up. I do not want to hear, A penny saved, a penny earned. I do not want a penny. I do not want to take it a little at a time. I do not want to put away a little bit every day for my children. I do not want to watch it accumulate bit by bit. I do not want a nest egg. I want a nest full of eggs. I want it all. I want to win. I want to win now.

40.

(Give Me My Damn Shoebox)

My head is clear. My mind is clear.

I am in control. I see numbers.

I see patterns.

I see amazingly elegant patterns, the kind of patterns that ought to win.

If you could just catch them like that, when they're about to come in, you would be set for life. All of the mistakes that you've made would be forgiven. When you're in a hole this deep, the only way to dig yourself out is the way you dug yourself in.

This is true. This is true. This strikes me as so true, my teeth are chattering.

I can't sleep. My mind is clear.

These people are crazy. How can they tell me not to gamble? If I don't gamble, how can I save myself from what gambling got me into? How can I make it right?

This is so true, I sit up. I've got the chills. My mind is clear.

I want that shoebox.

They want to take my house, they want to destroy my family, and I'm supposed to just let them because they are the law? But if I went out right now and banged the big machine, the new one, at $40 a pop, and brought home a check for $200,000, what would they do? *Not* take it because I earned it gambling? Of course they would. I owe them money, not obedience. I am not some little kid they can tell what to do. If I hit the big one, they would take their little bit, their taxes, their back taxes, their bankruptcy buyout, and then leave me the hell alone.

This is so true. I am reaching under the bed. It's my shoebox and I want it. What is the point of having it and not using it when there is all of that free money in the casinos—

One part of me is trying to be quiet and secretive about it. The other part, the involuntarily chattering teeth part, the so true part, doesn't give a damn about quiet. It's my shoebox and it's in my hand. I'm pulling on some pants, a shirt, the shoes I had on yesterday. The chattering teeth part of me doesn't care whether my socks match. The chattering teeth part of me doesn't care that the ex-wife has been awakened by the noise and is sitting up in the bed. The chattering teeth part doesn't care about her sobs in the darkness.

It's so true. It's so true. I just want to get out that door. My mind is clear.

I don't want a scene. I just want to get in that car with my shoebox, hon.

She is out of the bed. Her arms are holding me back. She emits a piercing cry. She pleads, "Let's talk about this. Let's talk. Don't do this!"

"But I'm doing it for *you*."

"I don't want it! I don't want that devil money!" She is a wild woman in the dark. Holding me. Hitting my chest. Holding me. Screaming so loud like howling. The boys are going to wake up. The boys must already be up. "I don't want it! I don't want it!"

I hear a noise out in the hall. It is one of the boys. Maybe all of them. I don't want my children to see this.

I break away.

I'm out of that house so fast. In the car. Cranking the engine. She is sitting on the ground with the front door wide open behind her. Head down in her hands. Loud sobbing noises coming from her. In her pretty underwear. How happy she will be when I bring home that big check!

This time I'm going to let her handle all of the money.

Let her handle it. That's the key. She is the responsible one. Let her give me an allowance to gamble. That way the bills will always be paid. The water will never be turned off again. She will be treated like a queen.

A light goes on in the house. My youngest son appears behind her.

My allergy boy. I can't let him see me like this. He knows me better than the rest. What is he trying to say to me? He's holding up his hands. He's waving. He's doing something with his fingers. Two fingers on one hand. Three fingers on the other. Is this a sign, Lord? He's the luckiest child in the world.

My wife is getting up. She's coming to the car in her pretty underwear. I am gone. I am out of there.

Wish me luck, hon.

41.

(You've Got to Be in It to Win It, It's All or Nothing, Baby)

I have a sense of destiny. I feel that something big is going to happen. I am seeing elegant patterns. I have $600 in my shoebox.

At 40 bucks a pop, that is at least 15 pushes.

A gambler is nothing if he is not an optimist.

You've got to be in it to win it.

I am going to be in it.

42.

It's just like anything else in America.

Nobody wants to hear your excuses about why you lost.

They want you to win. Go out there and win. You bring home the big check, we don't care how you got it. Steal. Gamble. Kill. Just bring it home.

It's the same as any other game—you can't let them beat you. You can't give up. If the pitcher strikes you out, you try your best to slap a home run the next time at bat. If he strikes you out again, you go right back out there and face him down again. You don't give up. You keep on slugging.

It's not always about losing. I've been down to my last dollar and hit jackpots. I've walked out of the casino resolving never to return, then suddenly turned around with the last dollar in my wallet and hit a jackpot. That has happened more than a few times. You can't give up. America is no place for quitters and whiners. You've got to keep on trying until you win. America accepts only winners.

When I reach the casino, I breathe a prayer. Lord, please help me. You know that I've done wrong, but I'm ready to do right now.

The cameras at the entrance remind me that I am not in disguise. Somewhere upstairs in the control room there is a list with my name on it. Some computer thing is accessing the file they have on me. My time is limited. It won't be long before they come to get me. But I know the score: If I win, I win.

The money is still mine.

The best they can do is say, Now, P, you know you're going to get us fined for doing this. But the money is mine.

I've seen it happen. I've seen them kick a barred gambler out of here with a check for $20,000.

It's not too crowded tonight. I go to the 40-buck bank and select an end machine because I've observed that the ones that begin and end a row hit more often. I deposit the entire $600 into the machine. No guts, no glory. I set my screens to 2-3-2-3-2-3 and 3-2-3-2-3-2 (in honor of Junior and because my allergy boy held up two fingers and then three and because today is the 23rd day of the month) and 7-3-7-3-7-3 and 3-7-3-7-3-7 (in honor of my mother, who was born March 7, 1937). I hesitate a moment before pressing the MAX BET button.

No guts, no glory.

My heart is beating out of my chest.

I press *PLAY*.

It comes up 3-7-3___. FIRST-THREE. Yes! Yes! At 40 bucks a push, I have hit $600 on my first push. Yes! My *TOTAL* now reads *$1,200*.

I press *CASHOUT*. I take my money in hundreds. I put it in my wallet. I go to the bathroom and rest on the toilet. I've been there only a few minutes and I'm already up $600! That's more than I make in a week driving the bus.

I have won. I have beat them. I can sneak out of here now and stick this in my shoebox. I am a winner tonight.

I go back out, and my end machine is still available. I am a winner tonight. I have already won. I can leave. I can go home a winner.

I have a better idea.

I put $600 in the machine and keep $600 in my wallet. No matter what happens, I win because I'm playing with their money now.

MAX BET. Forty bucks a pop. Fifteen pushes between me and everlasting glory.

After 15 pushes, my *TOTAL* reads $0.00.

Unbelievable.

It did not hit once. Not once. Not even one time? Is that even possible?

I go back into the bathroom and ask the mirror, How? How? How can a machine go 15 pushes and not hit once? Not once. No ANY-THREE. No ANY-TWO. No FIRST-ONE. Nothing. Nothing. That is so unlikely. It defies all odds. Just give it a rest. Let the bad luck run out of it. Give it a rest. At least I still have my original $600.

I give it a rest.

When I leave the bathroom, the end machine is still available. I take out my wallet and deposit $320 from my remaining $600. I am full of hope. I am all hope.

But no, the thing cleans me out.

I am down to my last push.

The *TOTAL* reads $40. I push *PLAY*. The balls bounce across the screen, 9-8-9-8-2-2. The *TOTAL* reads $0.00.

I am back in the bathroom again talking to the mirror: It has to hit something. It defies all odds. It's not hitting anything. It's taking my money . . . I worked so hard week after week at 40 bucks a day to get it up to $600. All I got left is $280. Lord, come on. Give me a break. Stop doing this to me. Come on, cut me some slack. Please, Lord. Please. I really need this. How can I go home tonight if I lose all this? What will I tell her? Bless this $280, Lord. Bless this $280.

When I leave the bathroom, the end machine is still available. I take out my wallet and deposit $200. I press *PLAY* five times at $40 a pop.

In the end, my *TOTAL* reads $0.00.

"Damn. You have got to be kidding me. Is this machine broken or something?"

But I'm no punk. I'm not letting any damn *ping-ping* machine punk me. I take out my wallet and deposit the remaining $80. I lower my bet to $10. Eight pushes, I tell myself. Eight pushes between me and ever-lasting glory.

I close my eyes. I press *PLAY* seven times. The machine is singing a lot as I push. I'm excited as hell. *Ping-ping-ping*. I can't wait to open my eyes. I open my eyes. Sigh. My *TOTAL* reads $612.

Okay, so I've made my money back. Actually, I've made $12.

This is a joke. This place is a real joke. They're trying to drive me crazy. If I leave here now, I am up $12. I left my family in the middle of the night for $12?

Screw you, Indians. Screw you, machine. Hit something, damnit!

I hit *MAX BET*, close my eyes, and press *PLAY* 12 times. There is no singing at all. I open my eyes. My *TOTAL* reads *$132*. "There is no logic to this thing. No logic and no God! You hear me?" I say out loud as I lower my bet to $10. "Thirteen pushes between me and everlasting glory. Bless it, Lord. Bless it. Do it."

I close my eyes and press *PLAY* ten times. There is no singing as I push. In fact, it is so quiet that I open my eyes to see just what the heck is going on. My *TOTAL* reads *$32*.

Nothing. Nothing. Nothing. Nothing. Nothing. Nothing. Nothing. Nothing. Nothing. How is that possible? It defies all logic. It defies all odds. They took my $600 and left me with $32.

I have hit nothing.

Nothing.

What's even worse is, I see the floor people coming toward me. Three of them, plus a burly Indian security officer. There is purpose in their steps. Yeah, of course they would recognize me *after* I lost my money.

I quickly raise my bet to $32, which is all I have left, minus the gun in the shoebox in the car.

The floor people are upon me.

"P, right?"

"No, that's not me. I don't know anyone by that name."

"Yes you do. You're P. We know you. You're not supposed to be in here."

The big security officer clamps a hand on my shoulder.

I press *PLAY*.

43.

I am weeping in my car.

44.

I am weeping. I am weeping. I am in my car. I am praying to God through my weeping. God is a good God. I love God. I love Him so much.

I am weeping. I am praying to my God.

I know I let You down. I know I let everybody down. I do not deserve Your mercy. I do not deserve Your forgiveness. But I ask for it. I ask that You forgive me. Forgive me for being weak. Forgive me. Forgive me. Give me the strength. Give me the strength, I pray as I remove the loaded cartridge from the gun. I take out the citation that the Indians gave me:

. . . you have been found in flagrant violation of the Gaming Code of the State of Florida . . . further infraction shall result in your arrest and a fine of $5,000 in accordance with state statute . . .

I tear the official-looking paper into shreds and sprinkle them over the unloaded gun, then set the lid on the shoebox. I look out the window at the casino. I say goodbye for the last time. I am weeping. I am weeping from sadness. I am weeping from joy. *Ping-ping!* My nest is full of eggs.

Oh, Mom, you would be so proud of me.

45.

My wife, my ex-wife, is in a housecoat at the kitchen table.

The boys are there, too.

There are plates on the table and cups. They've been eating a store-bought pie and drinking sodas. My ex-wife has been drinking something stronger. It's some strange kind of party. They are deciding something. About me, of course. She will not look at me, but the boys do. The boys look at me with sad eyes because they are not strong enough to look at me with hate.

I say to the boys, "Go to bed, guys . . . I mean, shouldn't you be in bed? There's school tomorrow."

They look to their mother, who signals them: It's all right, go. They go. Not a word to me. Not even my allergy boy, and it's all thanks to him in a way. He's the luckiest child in the world.

And she still won't look at me. She stiffens when I touch her.

I say to her, "Here's how it's going to be from now on. I'm going to GA tomorrow. I'm going every night. I'm going for as long as it takes. I'm going to church with you on Sunday. I'm going to be there for the boys more. I had to get it out of my system. I understand now that it's not a game. A game is something you can win if you try harder. Work harder. Play better. A game is fair. This thing, it's not fair. The rules are all in their favor. But it works on people like me, people who don't like to lose. The harder we try, the more *they* win, because it's not a fair game. And it's sick. If you win, what are you doing? Are you beating the house? No. You're beating other poor suckers just like yourself. That's whose money you're taking. The house has already taken its cut. I'm going to get it out of my system, I promise. I'm going to fix myself. I love you. I love the boys. I've hurt you all so much. I've hurt everybody I love. I sat tonight in the car with a gun. It was loaded. I was thinking about Junior . . ."

She looks at me for the first time. "I don't believe you."

"I'm telling the truth."

"I don't believe you." But she is looking at me hard, trying to figure it out. The change. She says, "Why are you smiling?"

If she only knew.

"Why are you smiling?"

Wait until I tell her.

"Why are you smiling?"

It defies all odds. I have beat the odds. God is a good God. God is the God of *Ping-ping*.

"Why are you smiling?"

"I'm going to smile for the rest of my life, and you're going to be smiling, too."

"How much?"

"The Lord—"

"You don't even believe in God," she says.

"I do. I do. God is real. God was real tonight."

She lowers her voice. "How much did you win?"

"Guess."

"I don't have time for games."

"Guess."

"No! Tell me."

"You're no fun."

"You ruined my credit. You destroyed my home. You humiliated me in front of my brothers and sisters. What do I have with you? Nothing. Just more pain," she says, exasperated. "Just tell me, or get out."

"Hon—"

"I can't go through this with you anymore. I'm so tired of this!"

She jumps up from the table. I grab her around the waist and hold her there. She struggles, but I am not going to lose her. I hold her, despite her struggling, and pass the check before her eyes, whereupon she ceases to struggle.

A woman who hates you but loves you at the same time will swoon when you pass before her eyes a check in the amount of $160,000.

She is holding it with both hands like a love letter.

"Here's the deal," I say. "That check is yours—well, after I pay the taxes on it, and the back taxes on the other one. The rest is all yours. Do what you want with it. I'm leaving it all up to you. This time it's going to be different. I can't be trusted with money. But don't you see? Smile, hon. Smile. We're rich. Rich. All of our problems are solved."

She turns to me now. No words pass between us, my ex-wife and me. She puts the check back in my hand.

I don't understand.

"Hon?"

"Get out."

46.

I am in the car now with the big check, the shoebox, the gun, and C.L., who has come to comfort me this dark night as only another gambler can, with her understanding ways and her desperate loving.

We are like teenagers, the way we do it, again and again without talking, without thinking. She says Yah, yah, yah as we do it, like the sound you make when good cards fall. I am crying on her shoulder. We're crying on each other's shoulders with joy. It is so painful you wouldn't believe. We have to stop and just hold each other. Then we stop doing that, too. Her hair is a mess and the car smells. She puts her T-shirt back on and lights a cigarette as I fiddle with the radio and see for the first time the tattoos on her pale thighs. I hadn't noticed before, the dragon, the eagle. Perhaps she is studying me, noticing things on me for the first time. Perhaps she is wondering, as I am, Who is this person whose fluids have mingled with mine? What of pregnancy? What of disease? C.L. looks to be maybe 25. She exhales and rolls the window down, fanning the smoke. She asks to hold the check again, and I pass it to her. She peers down at it, studying it, in the semi-darkness of the car.

"Sweet Jesus."

"Sweet is right. And it would have been even sweeter if the bastards had let me hit when I was banging it at 40 bucks a pop."

"Oh, you were banging it, you were *banging* it!"

"I was banging it. You should have been there. You should've seen it. I was banging it. Sweet. Sweet."

"Forty bucks a pop. You don't hold back. Oh, you are amazing. You go all the way."

"Oh, it was beautiful. I knew that damned 3-2-3-2-3-2 was going to hit. I knew it. I just knew it. You know how it is when you just know it?"

"I know how it is. I know how it is. Oh, this is amazing. Sweet. Sweet."

"Oh, it is sweet. Damn sweet."

My ex-wife will come to her senses tomorrow, or the next day, or next week. She will get in touch with me then. She will see that what we have is too good to let go. She will celebrate my victory. She will see things as she should. All this money I'm carrying around, if she's not there to manage it for me, I'll only blow it, right? That's what she will think. For example, I already promised C.L. a big chunk of it to help her get back on her feet. To help her pay back her boyfriend. And she has promised to hang out with me, to be my pusher again.

Sweet.

Jesus.

I still love my wife. But it's okay. It's better than the darkness. It's better than suicide. I have been there and I know. There is nowhere else to go. You are up against a wall. There are walls on all sides. You need money, but you have none. Well, you have just a little bit, so you gamble with it to make it grow, but it gets smaller when you lose. So you have to get more money and make that grow to replace the bundle you just gambled, but they're turning off your water, so you have to give them something to keep it turned on, but then you have nothing to gamble with. So where do you get the money to gamble *and* pay bills? You need to gamble so that you can be happy. If you want to be a gambler, here is what you have to learn: You must surrender all other forms of joy. Only gambling equals happiness. Not paying bills. Not work. Not family. Not love.

Two uniformed security officers, doing their rounds of the casino parking lot on bicycles, make another close pass by the car. They cannot see inside because of the dark tint on my windows. Maybe they can. C.L. is snuggled against me, tenderly kissing my neck, saying, Oh, oh, you were banging it. My hand snakes under her T-shirt. Her flesh feels new and exciting. I press my lips against hers again. We are so hungry for it, this joy. We are tasting it in each other. The casino looms bright and beautiful in the distance on this glorious night. I cannot go back in there, but I am happy now with this check and with C.L.'s lips against my lips, and there are other places that I can go.

I want my wife and my family, but I am happy now.

I have $160,000, and I am happy.

My name is P, I am a gambler, I am lucky, and I am happy.

This is the ultimate.

This is joy.

I am on my way.

PART II

PROFESSIONAL

Vegas

I have a notion that gamblers are as happy as most people, being always excited. Women, wine, fame, the table—even ambition, sate now and then; but every turn of the card and cast of the dice keeps the gamester alive: besides, one can game ten times longer than one can do anything else.

—Lord Byron

This is the ultimate. This is the joy. Vegas is heaven.

—P

47.

That first day we get turned around trying to find Harrah's and end up downtown, where they say the sleazy joints are.

I go into the Gold Nugget. Is this sleazy? It doesn't look sleazy to me. What do I know? I'm from Miami. It looks fabulous. I am in heaven. I peel off a grand for C.L., who heads directly for the machines. Our bags are still in the car, I have a three-day growth of beard, I'm wearing yesterday's shirt, and I spy the Texas Hold'em room, where they've got all the antes you could ever want: quarter, dollar, $5, $20, $50, $100. A $1,000 ante. Oh lordy.

Tell me Vegas is not heaven. Tell me Vegas is not hell.

I've got sweaty palms. I've got goose bumps. I hear God talking to me. And He's saying, High-stakes poker.

I hear you, Lord. Preach it!

I stroll over to the $100 pit. God or no God, that's about as much as I am willing to risk after being eaten on the riverboats in the $20 games. Did I tell you about the riverboats? New Orleans and Biloxi, I'm trying to forget. New Orleans and Biloxi, that's the chapter I left out. God was talking to me then, too, and the boats took 25 grand from me in a little over a month. A seat is available. My heart is beating out of my chest.

I have five grand in chips stacked next to me. My stack is the shortest at the table—oh me, of little faith. There's over a million dollars in chips at this table. These are the big boys—they come to play. Every mouth is chomping something—cigarette, cigar, tobacco, gum, toothpick. Every head, except mine, has a hat or cap, most of them worn backward or cocked to the side. The dealer's a strange-looking man. He's got gray hair, gray eyes, gray eyebrows, and white skin one shade short of albino. When he calls for antes, he gives the word *expressionless* new meaning. But I'm not fazed by it. I've seen worse.

Hundred-dollar-ante poker. I can afford that. It's only money. Let's get it on, ugly white-face man. Deal me my first cards in Vegas.

He deals me in. I look in the hole.

Ace-ace.

I've got pocket rockets!

But don't let it show. Frown at them. These guys are pros.

I reach into my pocket for a mint. The cocktail waitress is swishing by. She catches my eye. No. Nothing for me, li'l lady, I grunt.

The bet's coming around. Four guys go down. Four guys are still holding, plus me and the guy after me. It's my turn now. I'm tempted to raise, but I don't. Cigarette raises to $800. Cigar calls. Toothpick calls. Gum and Tobacco fold. I'm tempted to raise my aces, but I just call.

The flop comes six, king, ace.

I've got trip aces! Jesus-Jesus-keep-me-near-the-cross.

Cigar's got the bet. He's looking Cigarette straight in the eye. Cigarette's looking right back at him. It's testicle against testicle in here today, boys. Nobody's looking at me. Cigar bets two hundred. Toothpick folds.

My turn. I'm tempted to raise, but I just call. Munching my mint. Swallowing hard. Digging in my pocket for another. Don't mind me, fellas, I'm just a mint-munching fool. (With unbeatable trip aces!)

Now it's Cigarette's turn, and he does not hesitate. He raises to a thousand right away. Cigar sits back in his seat. Fiddles with his chips. But he's still staring straight at Cigarette. Another drink lady swishes past. Cigar says, I see your thousand, I raise you another thousand. He pushes in his chips.

I'm tempted, tempted, so tempted to raise. But I munch my mint and just call. Maybe I called too quick. Now Cigar and Cigarette are looking at me. Me with my little stack of chips. Munching my mint. Digging in my pocket for more mints.

Who is this bozo?

Munch. Munch. Munch. I've committed $2,800 to the pot already, so my stack looks pretty sad next to theirs.

Then I get one of those moments. My brain is saying, Wait a minute, wait a minute, wait a minute. A little over a month ago, you would've banged $2,800 in maybe a couple days of gambling—now you are banging it in one hand. My oh my, P, how you have grown.

Cigarette reads me wrong and says, Re-raise $2,000. Cigar grunts, but then calls.

It's my turn again. Munch. I call. Munch. Munch.

They both look at me like I'm an idiot. All I have left of my stack is two hundred dollars. They're thinking, If he had something, then he should have just raised it all-in. Jheeze, what a bozo.

I'm thinking, What a bozo I am, I should have raised it all-in. I have an unbeatable hand. But it's only $200. Munch. Munch.

So now they're not looking at me anymore. I don't matter to them. I'm just a mint-munching bozo.

The next card comes, the turn card, and it's a seven, with no chance for a flush, since all of the suits are out. Cigar checks. Cigarette bets a thousand.

Munch. I throw my last meager two hundred in and announce, All-in. Munch. Munch.

Old Cigar has seen enough. He folds. The dealer gives Cigarette back his change from the all-in, and then puts the river card out there. It's a deuce. It's no help for Cigarette, though he is smiling—he must really have a great hand. He can't wait to show bozo his great hand.

But what he doesn't know is that there's no way for bozo to lose. Trip aces is the best hand possible, and bozo has it. Poor Cigarette.

He shows his hand.

Pocket kings: He has trip kings. It was a good hand. A monster!

I show my hand. Pocket aces: trip aces. A bigger monster! Ha.

Cigarette curses under his breath, then nods his head in surrender as the dealer pushes me the pot. I don't count it, but there's got to be close to 15 grand in there.

All around the table I hear, Good hand, good hand, as I tip the dealer.

My first hand in Vegas, and I win it with trip aces. The nut. An unbeatable hand.

But, as they say in church, the Lord ain't finished with me just yet. My second hand is also the nut. An ace-high flush in clubs.

Preach it, Lord! Preach it!

When I look down at my chips again, I have about 30 grand—close to 25 grand in profit. In two hands in Vegas I have just made up all of the money I blew from two weeks in Mississippi and a month in Louisiana on those lousy riverboats. Vegas is great. Vegas is home. I was born to play in Vegas.

The day rolls on. In no time, I am up nearly $100,000.

You would think I play here all the time. My stacks are as high as anybody else's at the table. I'm scared to count the chips the stacks are so high. I have never seen so much money. Is all this money really mine? I came here expecting a beating, but now the feeling of doom has been lifted. All my problems can be solved with just what's contained in these stacks.

And the other players—the way they're all looking at me. Who is this guy? Where'd he come from? Where'd he learn to play so good? They fear me. They hate me. I'm taking all of their money.

I am their target. I am the one they want to beat.

But it ain't gonna happen. I'm playing by the rules. Be patient. Wait for the good hands. Fold the bad hands. Play the players. Look for signs in their faces. Look for signs in their twitches and grunts. Look for their tells. Wait them out. Good players are patient. You are one of the good players, P.

I get up from the table and stretch my legs. I need to pee. I need a pack of mints. I look back at my seat and admire my chips. I can't believe it. My stacks are now the highest at the table. Nice. All of that money I spent on machines trying to get *less* than this. What was that all about? This is so . . . easy. My bags are still in the car. My original five grand is gone, thanks to C.L., who has come back enough times to clean it out banging the machines. But I am hot, man. Hot.

When I sit back down, I give a friendly smile to the other gamblers with their cigars and their gum and their turned-around hats. They hardly smile back. I offer them each a mint. No one accepts. But that's all right. No hard feelings. I don't need your friendship, I just need your chips. Keep 'em coming, fellas.

At some point, I take a longer break to find C.L. I give her enough cash so she can get us squared away with a room. I give her a few more bucks to hold onto so she can bring me back a little food from time to time while I'm sitting at the table. Man shall not live by mints alone. The best gamblers never eat at the table, I know; eating gives off too many tells. But I'm new at this and I'm hot and I don't want to risk leaving the table for too long because my seat might get cold.

And it continues, with food or without. I win. I win. I win. And when I lose, the others celebrate. But I lose less often than I win. I lose less money than I win.

Late in the day, Cigarette finally beats me with a full house (I had the ace-high flush on the flop—tough break for me), and he shouts, I finally got you! Ha.

I glance down at the quarter of a million in chips sitting in front of me, and say to him, Good hand. Good hand.

But can't he see?

I'm just a guy. Why come after me? Just play the cards. Why spend a hundred grand trying to beat me? A hundred grand . . . oh what a fool you are, Cigarette. Ha.

By the time I leave the table on that first day, my profit is close to $300,000. More money than I won in my big jackpot. More money than I have ever won in my life. Let's see, at $10.64 an hour as a bus driver—yep. That's more money than I earned in all of my years of driving a bus.

How sad. Bus drivers do noble work. So do teachers. And police officers.

But I am a gambler, and my stacks are so obscenely high they're leaning.

The other players can't figure me. I throw away most hands—20, 30, 40 in a row—yet I catch a lot of monsters. Nut flushes. Nut trips. Nut straights and full houses. What they don't know is that I bluff a lot, too. I have won more than a few hands with nothing in the hole. (3-7 ha! take that!) I'm playing the players, baby. When you're hot, they don't want to test you.

It will not always be like this, I know. The cards are as fickle as fate. There will be bad days, I know. But today is not one of them.

It is my 17th hour at the table. C.L. is over my shoulder, saying in my ear, Come to bed, baby. Come to bed. Let me show you our room. Her tongue flicks lightly in my ear.

Well, there is always that.

The fruits of my labor.

48.

The next day I win again. I've got more money sitting with me at the table in chips than I earned in my entire life, plus my wife's salary, too.

The next day I win again. Am I a millionaire? Is it possible? Let me count it one more time. There it is—one million dollars in chips.

So I go out and buy the cowboy hat.

A legend's got to have a trademark. A black hat to show I take no prisoners.

It's a real nice hat.

I can afford it.

49.

Win, win, win. In Vegas, I have the golden touch. In Vegas, I cannot lose.

At least that's how it goes the first year.

It Hurts Nothing

50.

I have a dream that I'm talking on this huge black phone too big for my head.

My mouth is full of cotton when I try to talk, I'm frantic, I'm weeping. I'm saying, I'm sorry. I'm sorry. I can't stop. I'm sorry. I'm sorry. I'm sorry. Every day I do this. There is no end. I don't even want to win anymore. I win—I want to give it back. I lose—same thing—I want to lose more. I just want it to end. I just want to get that monkey off my back. Maybe I should dump it all on the roulette wheel. Bet black. Let it spin. Win big or lose big—it's over. C.L. won't let me. C.L. won't let me. Good old C.L. Why did I say that? I really miss you, hon. I do.

Too late, she says.

Give me a chance.

You need help, she says.

Give me another chance—

You and your C.L.

It's not about her, honey, don't hang up, it's not about—

What do you want your coffin to look like?

My coffin?

What do you want your coffin to look like?

But it's not my wife's voice anymore. It's a scary voice. Evil-sounding. It sounds like the voice of the devil. It spooks me so much I hang up the phone. I will myself to wake up. I awaken to the cold and dark of my room. It's freezing cold. It smells bad, too. I roll over and there's a man lying in bed with me. He's looking at me with yellowed eyes. His black face is deformed like someone who has been in a bad accident. His teeth are so long they reach down to his knees. He reaches for me with skeletal fingers, and I awaken again. It was another dream.

This time I awaken to real life. I am in my room. I am lying in my bed next to C.L. Strange.

This happens two nights in a row.

51.

I am lying to C.L. about money more and more these days. How can I not have money? She sees what's happening at the table, and she bitches and bitches about it. She sees my chips stacked up. So how can I say I have no money? She's absolutely right.

What she cannot see is what is happening to herself.

I give her a grand when she gets up in the morning. She comes back for another at noon. She needs at least two grand at night. That's a good day. She has had several ten-grand days. Even with the kind of money I'm pulling in at the tables, a ten-grand day is a bad day.

You're treating me like I'm some damned child, and I am not a child, she says.

She's right about that.

Did I think, once upon a time, that she was 25? Try 35.

But when she's hot, she's hot. She has hit several jackpots of 20 and 30 grand so far. She has a knack for sensing a machine that's about to hit. But where does the money go? Right back into the machine.

Ah, C.L.

She loves me. But she's married to the machines.

So I keep the petty cash locked in the safe. She has a bank card that I load whenever she needs more, but she has to come to me to ask, and she does not like that. It's just a two-minute phone call and the card is loaded, but boy she hates to ask. Begging, she calls it. Begging my nigger. She doesn't mean anything by it. She has that kind of temper.

I catch her one night trying to crack the safe with a bread knife.

That is the same night she hits me.

Now dig this. She loses a grand, not me. She comes up to the room and holds out the card. I say, with no sarcasm at all, Maybe you need to cool it for the night. Take a rest. And she up and hits me right in the face. So I hit her back, not too hard, but just to let her know not to do that. And she calls the cops on me. Tells them that I got rough with her.

Can you believe this crazy girl?

So they take me downstairs to the hotel manager's office. What's this all about? We can't have this here, they warn. We like you, P, you're a good guest, but you need to learn to control your woman, they explain.

I will, I will, I promise them.

They offer coffee. I take the coffee.

Then I tip everybody a hundred. The cops get two.

A half hour later I open my door, and she's trying to stash the bread knife in her pants after picking at the safe with it. You can see the nicks in the metal around the dial.

I take the bread knife away, put it in the drawer with the other utensils, pick up the phone, and load two grand on her cash card. C.L.

says, Sorry, I'm so sorry, then kisses me tenderly. I kiss her back. I want to hold her in my arms a little bit longer, but she's out the door. Gone downstairs to her real lover, the machines.

But life is fabulous. Just fabulous. Really, it is. These days, two grand doesn't set me back at all. It hurts nothing. I'm still up. Way up. Let her have it, I tell myself. You know how it is. You've been there. Stop treating her like a child. I am at the window looking down on the night, at the fluorescent lights on the strip, at the people crowded shoulder to shoulder. My ex-wife calls.

Hey.

Hey.

Good to hear from you.

Yeah.

How you doing?

Fine. You?

Fine. Fabulous. The boys?

Fine. Your girl there?

I got lots of girls. What girl?

The white girl.

She's downstairs.

I saw y'all on TV.

Yeah. That spot. They run it on cable.

She looks good . . . I got a good look at her. I recorded it.

Erase it. *You* look good.

In case I need to kick her ass one day, I need to know what she looks like.

Ha-ha. Go on with your bad self.

Well, good luck to you.

Don't hang up. Don't go.

I just called to wish you luck on the tournament.

Thanks. I should have won last year. But it's tough.

Even for you?

Yeah. I'm running out of chips. I don't think I'm gonna win this year either.

I wasted my good luck wish, then.

Luck is never wasted.

You should know. You're a lucky gambler.

Hon . . . I had a dream about you.

Hmmm. Was I naked?

Hmmm . . . hmmm . . . Hey, you know, if you need anything, just say.

I don't need anything.

I miss you.

Come home.

Come to Vegas. Bring the boys. Bring _____ (allergy boy).

No. Hell no.

Let's not fight. Please. I'm just kidding.

I'm not bringing them to Vegas. Ever. Bye!

When C.L. comes back up, it's like 3 in the morning. I am prepared to load her card again if she wants me to. Instead, she crawls into bed beside me. She holds me for a while, then tells me to roll over on my stomach. I do and she gives me the back rub massage kind of thing she does. Her tongue is on my neck a lot while she's doing it. Pretty soon we're going at it hot and heavy. I hear a noise, and I freeze. We are not alone in the room.

Did this crazy bitch sneak some guy in here to kick my ass and steal my money?

C.L. giggles, and the girl who has been sitting in the dark listening to us make out turns on the light. She is the redhead dealer from one of the other casinos who we met when we played there last week. She is C.L.'s way of making it up to me. She is still in her uniform. My favorite kind. Bow tie. Tuxedo top. Cummerbund. Tuxedo pants. Black spit-shined wingtips. But underneath: big breasts and a black velvet thong. C.L. knows I had my eye on this girl, who had dealt me really, really good cards. It is a great make-up gift.

The redhead climbs in between us. Everybody kisses everybody. There's lots of giggling. C.L. is stoned. The redhead is way stoned. C.L. takes her first. Then afterward, they both take me.

Ping. Ping.

Ping!

The next morning, I give them a couple grand each to go blow in the casino. I head downstairs and try my best. I'm good, but the cards are too fickle. I go all-in on a pair of kings. I get beat by trip deuces. I am out of chips.

After I am eliminated, I check with the judges to see how I did. This year I end up in 40th place.

Not bad for my second year in Vegas, but still out of the running. Life is just fabulous. These days, getting knocked out of a million-dollar tournament doesn't upset me at all. It's just another day.

It hurts nothing.

I get back upstairs—C.L. is gone and my room has been cleaned out. She got into the safe, too. Now that I think about it, she and that redhead weren't so stoned after all. They had been watching me as I opened it to break them off a little cash: 32 left, 23 right, 13 left . . . All of the petty cash is gone.

Twenty grand.

It hurts nothing. I should have given it to her. I would have.

I don't see C.L. for three months. My friends tell me she's up in Reno banging the machines hard. She and some longhaired motorcycle guy. Three months I don't see her. Then one day she's outside my door. Back in my bed. Like nothing's happened. She has lost weight. There is a new tattoo on her hand, a thorny rose. She has a black eye. She smells like unwashed skin and marijuana. She's back in my bed giving me one of her back rub massage things. She's crying tears on my neck as she does it. Sobbing desperately into my neck for me to forgive. Now we are making love. She doesn't explain where and who with. I don't ask why. It hurts nothing.

It hurts nothing at all.

52.

This is what I write—

Dear _____,

I want to tell you what I did when you sent it back. I got real pissed off and I came this close to calling my lawyer. I am really hurt that you continue to treat me this way after all that we have been through together. What are you trying to prove? I am a changed man, I swear. Do you know who paid for ____'s medical school? And _____'s eye surgery? And saved _____ them's house? I did. I want to do no less for my sons. That thing that I was, I am not that anymore. That was a long time ago. I have straightened up my act, I swear. I am a professional gambler. A PROFESSIONAL. These days I hardly even gamble at all, maybe fifty hours a week. I'm not bragging, but I am very good at what I do, and you need to understand that. Those boys are my sons. IT WAS A GIFT FROM

THEIR FATHER. A CHRISTMAS GIFT! Do not cut me out of their life. Don't force me to drag you into court because you know you would definitely lose. Oh yes you would. Get some sense into your head, woman. What are you trying to prove? I've tried to figure it out and I've come to the conclusion that something is just not right with your head. You need serious psychological help. As of right now, I am done with you. I've got better things to do with my time. Oh, and to answer your question: I could not be there because I was out of the country at the time for an important tournament. Christmas is just a holiday! Read my lips. It is my job! It is what I do! Stop poisoning my children against me!

—but I don't mail it.

Inventory of the Monkey

53.

One night we're at our casino and C.L. heads to the blackjack area. I'm surprised.

This is not her thing. The machines are her thing. She's not very lucky at cards, she claims. She finds card games slow and unexciting. But here she is laying down a hundred on blackjack. She seems to know what she's doing. Hit me, hit me, now stay, she says. And *bang, bang,* the cards fall her way. Soon, she's up a grand. She sits out a few hands, then she comes back in and lays down the grand she just won. She wins again. Now she's up two grand. She wins the next three hands—hit me, hit me, stay—now she's up 16 grand.

I am amazed.

I lean over her shoulder to congratulate her with a kiss, and she recoils. "See? I don't need anything from you."

She collects her money and goes over to the machines, where she promptly loses six grand back. She returns to the blackjack table with the remaining 10 grand. Hit me, hit me, stay, she says. Now she's up to 40 grand.

"Amazing," I tell her.

She says, "I'm going to be richer than you pretty soon. You'll see."

"But we're not competing. We're a team."

"That's what you call it."

"Hey now—"

She shrugs away from my arm. "Leave me alone so I can concentrate."

Hit me, hit me, she says. Stay, stay, hit me.

The cards fall.

Over the next half hour, C.L. loses a few hands, but most of them are winners. She's grinning and cackling. I've never seen her so happy. She's got $300,000 sitting in front of her. A crowd has gathered. Gamblers like to see other gamblers bet it big. C.L. has placed her entire $300,000 on it. She's betting it big. Hit me, hit me, she says.

The dealer announces, 21!

C.L. wins again!

She leaves the table with $600,000. Everybody's applauding like crazy. The girl has instinct for the game, I hear someone say.

Up in our suite, C.L. is elated (and cocky) as she counts out her money.

"You were amazing," I say. "You took them good."

"Tomorrow night I'm going to take them even better."

"You seemed to know when to hit and when to stay."

"I got good instinct for the game."

"Do you? You used to hate cards."

She flips out on me. "You're jealous! You think only you can get lucky?"

"No, no," I say. She has taken it the wrong way. I don't want to fight. I want her to finish her counting, put the money in the safe, and then make love to me. I want to work on our relationship tonight. I want to remove the wedge that is being driven between us by her so-called support group. What do they think I am, her pimp? Is that what they tell her? Her sexist pig black man? It's not like that with us. I love her. We've been together a long time. We've been through a lot. She's not as crazy as she used to be, true, but I am the *man*, and it is my job to handle the money because C.L. is the only gambler in the world who without a doubt is a bigger degenerate than I am. If C.L. handled the money, we would have been broke and back in Miami a long time ago. She just doesn't know when to quit. But tonight—tonight I am proud of her. She won and she got up before she lost it all back. That is the key to luck. You have to learn not to abuse it. You have to learn to get up while you're ahead. Go to your room. Count your money. Make love to your man (make love to your man twice). Come back to gamble another day. "No, no," I say to C.L., "I don't think that way at all. I'm proud of you. I am lucky to be with you."

She's still a little snippy, but something in her melts.

I lick it all up.

Just the way she likes it.

We're going at it on the floor surrounded by her many, many stacks of hundred-dollar bills. I'm huffing and sweating and telling her how much I love her, how we are such a great team, how I am the luckiest man in the world because of the day I met her, how I want to make our union a more permanent one, how between the two of us we will win all the money in Vegas, all the money in the whole gambling world, after four years I think I know you, I know I love you, will you marry me, C.L., will you?

And she huffs, Yes, yes, yes, but is it about marrying me or about how deep I am up in her?

The answer remains suspended in the air as the door bursts open and casino management (accompanied by several officers of the law) enters our chamber of love and lucre, all of them waving badges and writs and showing guns.

An officer of the law recites: "C.L., you have the right to remain silent, you have the right to an attorney, if you cannot afford one . . ."

I have draped my body over hers to shield her from their intruding eyes. Beneath me, she begins to sob. I roll off my love, cease to shield her from their greedy eyes, which are not greedy for her at all, but greedy for and amazed at our stacks of money. *Yes, officers, it's real money. We got it like that. We are lucky gamblers.*

Well, at least I am a lucky gambler. C.L., casino management is informing me now, is an *unlucky gambler*. The cheating kind. Her dealer accomplice has already been arrested and has confessed.

The eye in the sky sees all.

Why did she do it? Why? She of all people knows that there are cameras all over the casino. She needed money, all she had to do was ask. That was the game plan. I have all the money she will ever need. She just has to ask. But no, she wants to do it on her own. Some kind of feminist crap I don't even pretend to understand that her friends have been putting in her head. Why does she need a support group anyway? She has me. Support groups are a crock. They are driving a wedge between us.

A female officer comes out of C.L.'s closet with a shirt and pants for her to wear. They allow me to help her dress. We are looking into each other's eyes, into each other's souls, through our tears. She touches my face. I kiss her cheek. No words are necessary when you have an understanding like ours. We are a team. She is led out of the suite in handcuffs.

Casino management and two officers, specialists, remain behind to collect the loot. One officer is making snide comments about the many, many stacks of cash they are fitting carefully into plastic suitcases. *So this is how you do it. So this is how you get to live, like this, Mr. Lucky Gam-*

bler. You cheat. Ha-ha. Cheating sure is one way to do it. Cheating sure beats luck any old day. Ha-ha.

He's mighty pleased with himself. Smart guy. I don't like him. I'm not in the mood for his smartness, so I let it slip. *That is $600,000 you got there, count it carefully or steal it, what do I care? I got like a million right here in my room safe. I got like three million in the casino vault. I got another five or six million somewhere in a couple of banks growing daily interest bigger than what you make in a year plus bribes. No offense, but this is chump change on the floor you're picking up, buddy. Six hundred thousand dollars. C.L. doesn't need this pocket change at all, and she is innocent until proven guilty. She can afford an attorney and she will get the best. She won't spend a day in jail, I promise you.*

I can see he wants to smack me, and if casino management weren't present, he would.

After they leave, I drive down to the jail. My lawyer's already there, already bailed her out. Twenty thousand dollars. Pocket change. She is still being processed for release while he's telling me how it's going to be.

Bad. They got her on tape. She was clumsy. They saw it all. Plus the dealer squealed like a pig. She's going to have to do some time.

I don't want her to do any time.

With the kind of money she took them for?

Chump change. You know how much I pay here in rent?

Chump change to you. To regular people, a jury of her peers, it's five years at least.

No time. I want her to beat this, understand?

Hmmm. Well, the dealer is the pro. C.L. was dragged along for the ride. It's going to be an uphill battle, but I'll do my best.

And I'll pull some strings.

Do your thing.

You do yours. No time, you hear me? I want her to beat this.

So that night, after she is released, we can't sleep in our hotel suite because she is being sued by their casino, so we go to this other place I own. The people renting it have some furnished rooms in the back with a view of the pool. We stay there for the night. C.L. opens the blinds so she can see the lighted pool, then falls into bed. I fall into bed, too, and hold her.

I don't ask her why she did it. That's not even the point. She did it because we have to work on our relationship. Get rid of the wedge between us. We are a team. A team has to act like a team. It should have been me and her stealing from the casino, not some redheaded dealer woman. I have to get through to her somehow. I have to. Maybe we should go to a casino. Blow some chump change. Relax a bit. Get our minds off this.

In the darkness, she suddenly says, "When I was in college, we had to read this story by Pushkin. I forget what it was called, but it was about gamblers. See, there was this gambler who used to go into the casino all the time and not play at all. He would just study the cards as they fell. Day after day he would do this. He was trying to come up with the perfect method for winning at gambling. But try as he might, he couldn't do it. He kept bumping into luck. Luck is random. There is no mastering it. There is no method. No trick. Then he heard about this old lady who, when she was young, had found a way. See, she had lost a lot of money gambling, then went to her husband and asked him to pay the debt, but he was tired of bailing her out, so he refused. The husband thought he was teaching her a lesson, but instead he was making her feel like . . ."

I hold her tight. "Go on."

"Well, a lecherous old prince heard of the woman's plight and told her that for a few nights of passion, he would teach her a secret trick to beat the cards. She gave him the nights of passion and he whispered the secret formula to her. Then she went back to the casino and won back all of the money that she had lost and then some. But now she was old and had never told anyone the secret trick. So what the gambler did was, he tricked the old lady's niece into getting him into their estate and then he went straight to the old lady's room and demanded to be told the secret to beating the cards. When she refused, he threatened her with a gun—and the old lady dropped dead of a heart attack. Then what happens is, her ghost comes back and tells him that she will give him the secret if he would promise to play it just as she told it to him, and then never to play it again. So he promised the ghost that he would. The old lady's ghost told him that the cards would fall as 3, 7, and ace. That he was to play one card on each night for three nights and then never play again. So the guy plays on the first night and bets a ton of money on 3, and it comes up. He doubles his money. On the second night, he comes back with his winnings plus most of his life savings, and he bets it on 7. Everybody in the casino is holding their breath as the dealer turns the card. It's a 7. The guy doubles his money again. He is now richer than a king. Then on the third night, he comes in with all of his winnings, plus every penny in the world he owns. He bets it all on ace. And to his and everyone's surprise, the card comes up a queen. The guy is freaking out. He can't believe that he lost every single cent he had in the world. Then he looks down at the card and sees that the queen the dealer turned over did not have the regular queen's face. Smiling up at him was the face of the old lady he had frightened to death. I remember the name now. The story was called 'The Queen of Spades.' I liked it a lot."

"Don't call me a spade," I joke.

She's real quiet. I think maybe she's falling asleep. Her head is resting on my chest. My chest is wet with her tears. It is late at night and we have to appear for arraignment tomorrow. Maybe a relaxing trip to a casino is a bad idea. Maybe we should just get some sleep.

I understand her story completely. The guy's a gambler. What gambler wouldn't kill to gamble? What gambler wouldn't kill to win? I mean, not me, but other gamblers. They would kill to gamble. I am lucky, so I don't have to, but others would do it, I'm sure. I think that's the point of the story, but maybe it's not.

One thing I do know is that the old lady is a bitch.

If she had this secret, why not tell the guy? Why not tell somebody? What good was it to her? She wasn't using it. Gambling is real hard on us, and if you know how to beat it, you should tell. It's not fair to keep a secret like that to yourself. Are you working for the casinos? They're the bad guy, not the poor gambler.

And the old lady's husband, when she was young—he's a bitch, too. He should have just paid the debt and shut his mouth. That's no way to treat your woman.

No way at all.

My lawyer (the best), he does his best.

And I pull my strings. Hard.

The trial lasts four days.

At the end of it, I have high hopes, but C.L. is found guilty and sentenced to six months in jail.

For my lawyer, it is a sort of victory. For C.L., it is a victory (the accomplice dealer got 15 years). For me, it is not.

I'm pissed with everyone: the lawyer (punk), C.L. (why did you do it, baby, why? *I wanted to beat them. Beat them like they always beat us.*

And you, the idea of topping you, of wiping that arrogant smile off your face, Mr. Lucky Gambler, it made my heart beat faster. But baby, we're a team. That's what you call it), and the casino (ungrateful bastards). All the money I dump into this place. Treating my woman like this. I move out the same day. Move across the street into another casino's presidential suite, where I settle in and then sigh:

Six months without her. Six months. Maybe I'll ask her to marry me again when she gets out.

Maybe I'll ask her to leave.

Kick her to the curb *(but we're a team, P. Oh, so now we're a team?).* Six months in jail. Twenty years barred from every casino in the state of Nevada. Twenty years. What good is she to me now?

I mean, I still love her, but she really is no good to me now.

Why did she do it? Why?

Ah, C.L.

54.

"It's all about roundness," the professor says.

It is the day after I put C.L. on the plane back home. It is a good day, relatively speaking. Yesterday was a bad day. Yesterday I won't talk about. C.L. didn't go easy. Can you believe that after all I've done for her she's threatening to sue me for palimony?

"A pre-pubescent girl is unattractive in the eyes of a normal adult male because she lacks roundness. She hits puberty and everything changes. She gets curves. Breasts. Hips. Fuller arms and legs. A bigger ass. Roundness."

The professor outlines an hourglass figure in the air with his hands and smiles confidentially. He is reclined in a patio chair by the pool.

He's got his shirt off and his dark shades on and he's nursing a strawberry daiquiri, but he is checking out every shapely, bikini-clad woman who passes by. It is good to see that he hasn't lost his sexual appetite in spite of his major financial setbacks. He's my guest this week out here in Vegas. I'm covering his room and meals. I've bankrolled him 20 grand to improve on in the casinos. If he wins, he pays me back. If he doesn't win, he's probably going to come begging for more. I hope he wins. I'm in a pretty sour mood because of C.L. and I would really hate to turn him down, because he is, after all, my mentor.

"This whole mating game, this whole seduction thing, all of this fascination with sex—it's all up to the woman, really. See, after puberty, the female attains her roundness, and then—" the professor stops mid-sentence.

Two really nice ones, Ms. Brunette in a tiger-striped two piece and her girlfriend Ms. Big-Breasted Blonde in white tube top and white shorts, come out and make a big giggling fuss of unfolding their chairs and positioning them in the ideal spots in the sun. There is lots of bending over and sighing and moving about and more bending over. When they get their chairs just right, Ms. Big-Breasted Blonde takes off her white shorts, revealing her thong bottom, and Ms. Brunette takes off her tiger-striped top, revealing two perfect medium-sized breasts that are nicely tanned right down to the nipple.

The professor ceases his narrative, as he and I both wait expectantly for Ms. Big-Breasted Blonde to take off her top, too. Please. Pretty please.

She doesn't. She just takes out her iPod, sticks the buds in her ear, and joins her topless companion in stretching out face-up on the lounge chairs.

The professor shakes his head, disappointed, as I nod my understanding. He picks up his daiquiri and slurps lustily through the straw. He says, "So now she is round and she has sexual desires. The *woman* has sexual desires, mind you, not the man. So she displays the curves to a man that she desires. What happens? He, having attained sexual maturity also, is inexplicably drawn to the roundness. He is not attracted to the woman, but to her roundness. Her roundness triggers in him a reaction that results in a temporary sort of male roundness, an erection. An erection, unlike a lubricated vagina, is a discomfort, not a pleasurable sensation. The male seeks, in the female, relief from this discomfort, and here's the rub. He must give her things of value in return for this relief. What does the male give her? First and foremost, he must give her pleasure. The sex act is pleasurable to the female, not the male. She receives pleasure because of the clitoris, which delights in the friction of rubbing; he receives only release from discomfort and only at the very end of the sex act. Second, the male must give her seed that will ultimately result in offspring. Third, he must provide for her and the eventual offspring—in the wild, I mean, in primitive times. But it's not much different today."

"So you're saying males don't have sexual desire?" I'm sitting next to him in my patio chair. I have a good view of topless Ms. Brunette. I am keeping my eye on her. I have an erection. "Are you gay, professor?"

"I am not gay," the professor says. "And, no, we males do not have sexual desire. We have a sexual reaction."

I whisper, "I am reacting right now to that brunette's nipples."

"I, too, am reacting. But I am not desiring, P."

"I think you're wrong. I think I'm desiring because I'm salivating. This is definitely desire, professor."

"You're reacting," he insists.

"Can't a man just be horny?"

"No! A man can only react!"

"Whatever. You're the one with the education." I shrug. "Well, I wonder if they're desiring us."

The professor glances at them and decides, "They're most likely teasing. They know that we are reacting, so they're teasing us. Torturing us."

He's right about one thing. This erection is torture. Hmmm. "So a woman who does not desire you, but knows that you *react* to her, can dangle her roundness in front of you in order to get valuable things from you."

"We seek *release from discomfort* in them. They seek *things* from us. Protection. Food. Shelter. Babies. Multiple orgasms. Money."

"Holy crap!"

"What?"

"You finally said something that makes sense."

"What?"

"The casino is a woman with roundness."

The professor nods sadly. "You got the wax out of your ears at last, my boy."

"I mean, most of what you say is B.S., no offense, but I get this. This, I get."

"I'm glad you get it."

"But I still like to screw."

"P, look. Oh my God." The professor nods his head in the direction of Ms. Brunette and Ms. Blonde, who, to our great delight, is slithering out of her tube top. Her breasts are awesome. Big. Soft. Roundness.

I say to the professor, "Well, I've made up my mind. I am going to fu— *get my release from discomfort*, as you put it, from one or both of those women tonight."

"It's going to cost you."

"It always costs me," I quip.

I am getting up now so that I can go over and get this thing started, and the blonde has already scoped me out and is pretending that she hasn't, pretending she hasn't licked her lips ever so lightly in my direction. In fact, she is busy rubbing tanning oil on the shoulders and chest of the brunette—rubbing tanning oil all around and over those already tanned breasts. Such teasers they are. My penis has fully and completely reacted to their roundness. I am really going to enjoy the hell out of them. We're going to gamble and screw and gamble. Get my mind off C.L. But where are my manners? I have company over. Ever the good host, I say to the professor, "You want some of this?"

He says, "Naw. I better head to the casino and try to do something with this bankroll you spotted me."

"I hear you, man. Good luck." I slap him five.

He says to me, "Thanks for the loan, my friend, and good luck to *you* with your adventure."

"Yeah."

But for this adventure, I don't need luck. Just cash and a good stiff reaction to roundness.

55.

There is a time in every boy's life when his father is the greatest person in the world. I do not remember ever feeling that way about my father. Maybe he pushed me too hard. Maybe he didn't push me hard enough, who knows?

He wanted me to be a man's man, so he did things to toughen me up. These dark things I will not talk about, for he is, after all, my father.

Okay, there's one thing I will tell you. When he caught me smoking at twelve, he slapped my mouth so hard that he loosened a tooth. Then he dropped me off that night in the roughest part of town that he knew of—79th Street and Biscayne Boulevard—left me with five bucks, and told me to get back home how I could now that I was man enough to start smoking.

It was the middle of the night. I was a skinny—real skinny—12-year-old kid. As I made my way to a bus stop, every guy I saw—I thought he was a pimp or a pusher. Every woman was a hooker. Every unfamiliar sound was evidence of murder in progress. I wanted to believe that my father was still there. That he was close by, hiding in his car and watching to see how I would make out. Certainly he would not abandon me out here in this dangerous place. What kind of crazy man would do that to his son?

When I finally got home two and a half hours later, he was in bed snoring.

My father.

I remember his beer (Pabst Blue Ribbon), his beer belly, and his laugh, the few times I heard it. It was a good laugh. He bellowed. I wish I had heard his laugh more often. I remember that cowboy hat he always wore. It had small gold letters on the ribbon: *Don't Mess with Texas.* I do not believe that my father, who was born and raised in Miami, ever spent a day of his life in Texas.

I remember that he could be very patient with you when he wanted to be, like the time he taught me to ride a bike and I kept falling off. Even now, when I ride a bike, I get the feeling he's running alongside me with his hand on the back of the seat keeping me from tipping over.

He could be very gentle with my mother. He always made her laugh. I remember he whored around on her a lot. They fought about this all the time, but never in front of us. We could hear them in the bedroom shouting—hear her shouting, hear him taking it with the occasional rhetorical questions back: Well, what did you expect me to do? She came after me. I'm a man. Am I not a man?

Sometimes they would go out to the car to have it out. We would peep through the blinds and see their mouths opening wide, their wild white eyes blinking rapidly, but we could not hear.

For all his problems, he worked hard all his life to keep a roof over our heads. I know that he had plans for all of us, though he didn't talk about them much. I remember that he cried when my big sister V got pregnant at 15. She was the smart one, the one who would go to college and come back an engineer and make us all proud—before she met that guy with the Corvette. While my mother was screaming her lungs out at V in the kitchen, bemoaning her *whoredoms*, as she and the Holy Bible called it, my father shook his head, got a beer out of the refrigerator, and went into the den to watch TV. When I went in there, I saw that his eyes were red and his face was wet. Wiping away the wetness with a hand, he asked me to bring him another beer. His voice sounded so pinched it could have been coming from a man half his size. My father was a big guy. When I brought him back the beer, he whispered to me, "She's gonna make it, though. You watch her. She's a damn good girl. She ain't no whore. Your mother's full of shit saying that." I said to him, "Mom's full of shit?" And he slapped my mouth so hard he rattled my loose tooth.

My sister V and the Corvette guy didn't last long. She had her baby, finished high school, went to college, and came back as an elementary school teacher. She met another guy, a teacher like herself—married him and had three more kids. V made out all right. My father was proud of her, though he never said it that I know of. That's the way he was.

When he was sick and only had a few more months to live, I was watching a Dolphins game with him one Sunday at his house. There had been more of us there to begin with, my mother, my wife, our children, but they had wandered off to other parts of the house to do other things, leaving my father and me, the only true football fans, sitting there in front of the TV with the game. Suddenly, I had one of those moments when I expected something special to happen.

Well, here was my father who was dying. How many more opportunities would he get to be alone with me, his only begotten son? If he had any great pearls of wisdom, or whatever, to pass on to me, here was his chance. He was laying back in his recliner. Only his face showed. He was covered from neck to feet in blankets and quilts by my mother, who believed she could keep him alive longer if she could keep him warm. He had his beloved Texas hat on his head. He reeked of Vicks VapoRub and camphor (my mother, again, believing she could keep him alive longer if she could keep his nasal passages clear). He noticed I was looking at him and made a face like, What do you want? Say it, so I can get back to the game. My father hated when people interrupted a game with needless conversation, especially when Marino was playing.

I said to my father, "Me and you were in here when V got pregnant, remember?"

"I remember," he said, nodding. "So what?"

"You had faith in her. You said that she would do all right. You said that getting pregnant wouldn't hold her back. You were right."

"She's a teacher. She did all right."

"You knew she would."

"I knew she would," he echoed. Then he said, "What the hell is this all about, P? The game's on."

"Did I do all right?"

"Oh," he said. It sounded like a sigh.

I said, "Did I do all right?"

He said, "You got a nice family. A house. You did fine. You did all right."

"Did I?"

He said, "Turn the volume up."

I had the remote. I turned the volume up.

He said, "I don't want nobody to hear this. To hear you getting all mushy like this, for God's sake. Don't let your boys hear this. They have to grow up to be men."

"Did I do all right?"

"I'm proud of you."

"Are you?"

"I'm proud as hell of you."

"Even though I could've done better?"

"You could still do better. This is America. The game ain't over until it's over. You could go to college and get a degree. There's still time. I never understood why you didn't do it in the first place. You were the smartest of all the kids. You had the best brain."

"But I did the least."

"I didn't say that. Don't you put words in my mouth. All I'm saying is it's your world. You can have anything you want with your brain, but you decide not to use it, so I say, okay, he doesn't want anything. But then I see you with the Amway, and the silly investment plans, and the get-rich-quick books, and I say, okay, so he does want something. Well, go out and get it. Show the world what you can do. We're all waiting."

"You think I should go back to college?"

"Yeah. Or start your own business."

"But I have the kids. I gotta keep food on the table. It's hard."

"So you drive the bus," he said. "Okay. But can't you take classes, maybe, one at a time? They let you do that, you know. Then in a few years you'll have your degree."

"It takes so much time. I'm running out of time."

"You're crazy. You're not running out of time. You're just a kid. Now me," he said, "I'm running out of time."

I said, with a straight face, because I wanted him to hold on, because I wanted him to have courage: "You're not running out of time, Dad."

He said, "Yes I am. I'm dying, boy. But I hope I don't die until I finish my class."

"Class? What class?"

"I'm taking a college class on the computer there."

The computer was set up on the table next to the TV. I had seen it there for the last six months or so and just figured he used it to play video games or surf the Internet for news headlines. But a class? My father?

"A class in what?"

"Greek mythology."

"Greek mythology! Ha!"

He said, "Greek mythology. I've always been interested. It's a good class. I'm learning a lot. I wish I had gone to college. If I could do it all over again, I would go to college. If I could do it all over again, I would give up the women and the drinking and the gambling and I would spend more time with the learning. Now turn the volume back down, quit this damned mushiness, and let a dying man watch his game in peace."

I turned the volume back down. Then I turned it back up.

"What now?"

"You would give up the gambling?"

"Yes."

"You gambled?"

He closed and then opened his eyes slowly. He said in a quiet voice, "I was a serious gambler, I'm ashamed to say. Your mother has some idea. She thinks she knows, but she's not even close to knowing how bad I was. I was good at hiding it. I was good at lying to her. But I could never catch any luck. I was an unlucky gambler. I was bad. How much I lost. What I lost could have bought this house three times. What I lost could have sent the three of you to college, no problem at all. I'm ashamed to say it, but it's the truth. I'm a big fake. I let you down. I let everybody down."

"No, Dad. It's all right. It's all right. You kept a roof over our heads."

"You have your mom to thank for that. If she didn't start stealing from me to pay the bills, the roof would have been taken away. Oh, I can't lie to you anymore. The roof was taken away. I hit rock bottom. I lost the house."

"You lost the—"

"I lost the house. I couldn't pay the mortgage. I couldn't pay the second mortgage. My friend K, you remember K? You called him Uncle K. He's not your uncle. You have a white uncle? But when you gamble, everyone becomes your friend or your uncle because everyone you know you have to borrow from. K and me, we were friends for years down at the docks where we worked. He was good with money. He didn't gamble. He had good credit. He really bailed me out that time. Saved my ass. When the bank foreclosed, he bought our house and let us live in it. We pay him rent. He's a good friend. A real good friend. He saved our house. He saved my face with my children. He saved my face with you. But when I die and when your mother dies, everybody will find out the truth about the house. They'll know I was a goddamned fraud. There's no inheritance."

"Dad—"

"I can't tell you not to gamble, son, because it's a manly thing to do. It's what we do. It's like drinking or smoking or chasing women. It's what we do. But if you haven't started, then don't start. If you're doing it, then handle your business, don't let it handle you. Don't let it go too far. Take what you can and get out. And don't tell me about it. I don't want to know about it."

"But Dad—"

"Please turn the goddamned TV back down so we can watch the game."

"But—"

"Please. Please. Please."

My father got his wish. He died two weeks after he finished his course in Greek mythology. When the grade came, it was an A-plus.

56.

(A Fourth Definition of Insanity)

When I told him t'fetch,
He buried his bone.
When I told him to sit,
He shit.
When I told him t'eat,
He runned away from home,
And I ain't never seen him nor since.

Meditation

A gambler is nothing but a man who makes his living out of hope.
                                                    —William Bolitho

A gambler is nothing if he is not an optimist. Why not win it all?
Why shouldn't it be possible to win it all?

                                                                —P

57.

(My Beloved Allergy Boy)

My son sends me a birthday card.

He never forgets my birthday, my allergy boy. He's in high school now. It's one of those made-up cards with lots of blank space that you can write in and say something special. There's a picture of a brown-faced father and son (drawn in cartoon) playing chess on the front. On the inside, the words are, HAPPY BIRTHDAY, DADDY. OH, AND BY THE WAY, CHECKMATE!

That's my boy.

In the white space, my son has written, *thanks for being a great dad, p.s., today's Cash-3 numbers will be 123, ha-ha, love always, your son.* Real sweet.

My father told us that one. He used to say it all the time. He called it his old stupid dog song. I think I understood it better after he told me he was a gambler.

As a gambler, I have a complete understanding of insanity.

I hit my first royal flush the day after my father died.

Of course, I play the numbers. Straight. I have to drive way up to Idaho to play because Nevada has no lottery. Ha-ha-ha—Nevada has no lottery—ha-ha-ha-ha-ha-ha-ha. So I put a grand on it.

Of course, it comes in. Straight. 1-2-3, just like that. I have just won $500,000 in the Idaho Pick-3. Seems like when you really don't need the money, you just keep on winning.

I call C.L. and tell her about it. She asks me to send it to her right away, she really needs it. Who can need $500,000 right away? So we get into a fight.

She hangs up on me.

I call back all night, but she never picks up. When I stop calling, the phone rings. It's C.L.

"You never really loved me."

"Yes I did. I loved you with all my heart, but you couldn't get that monkey off your back. What was I supposed to do, huh? Watch you destroy yourself?"

But she has already hung up. She hung up in the middle of the word "monkey."

I call back all day, but she never picks up.

That night, after my class— Yeah, the casino gives me money and comps to teach a bunch of tourists colorful, useless stuff about gambling. Yeah, imagine me as a teacher. But I like to talk. They like to listen. They like to dream about hitting it big like me. I'm a hero to them. With my diamond rings, my Rolex, my cowboy hat.

Like I was saying, that night after my class, this Australian guy is bothering me with theories about play and crap about addiction—stuff I don't really care about because it's *all* a bunch of crap, really. The truth is, you've got to be in it to win it. And if you're in it, you're probably going to lose big. And I'm telling him this to get rid of him, but he's a pest, following me down to the casino, then out to my car when I pretend I'm sleepy and going home (though I live in the casino, in the hotel upstairs). This is what happens when you do these damn classes. It must suck to be a real teacher. They couldn't pay me enough to do this for a living for real.

I turn to the Australian guy and say, "Look. Here's the deal. Gambling is a serious addiction and I don't want to be irresponsible. You look like a nice guy. I don't want to sermonize like the happy gang at GA, but I don't want to glamorize the thing either. There's enough of that going on these days on the Internet and TV. I make money gambling because I am lucky. It's pure luck that I earn what I earn. The best advice I can give you on gambling is my father's advice to me: If you haven't started, then don't start. If you're doing it, then handle your business; don't let it handle you. Don't let it go too far. Take what you can and get the hell out. And don't tell me about it. I don't want to know about it. In fact, I never want to see you again, buddy. Beat it. You're a pest and you talk funny. Stop bothering me. I swear I'm gonna call security on your Crocodile Dundee ass."

The guy goes away pissed.

Screw him.

I'm not in the mood to be nice. I've had a long, hard day. I've got to get some gambling in.

Then I remember my beloved allergy boy. I call him and thank him for the card. Thank him for the 1-2-3. I tell him, "This is just between you and me. Don't tell your mother. Please do not tell this to your mother. She would kill me. She hates me giving you guys stuff, but I'm sending the money home to you."

He squeals with delight. He's the luckiest kid in the world.

"But there's something you have to do with it. You have to put it in a secret account I don't know anything about, okay?"

"Okay." Still squealing.

"I'm serious. I don't know when I'm going to hit rock bottom. I want to make sure you guys are taken care of."

"Rock bottom? You're rich, Dad. Richer than all my friends' dads put together. You've even been on TV." Still squealing.

Kids. God bless 'em.

I miss being surrounded by them on the bus. I take it back—it must be great being a teacher. Maybe I should teach. Maybe I should write a children's book and teach them not to gamble.

Or teach them to do it right.

"Just promise me you'll do what I say."

"Okay, Dad," he says. "You can count on me."

"I mean it."

"Serious."

"And whatever you do, never, ever, ever start gambling, okay?"

"But we could be like a business. I could give you numbers to play."

"Stop kidding around."

"We could be a team."

"Stop making jokes. This is serious. Do what I tell you, okay?"

I can't make sense of his answer for all the squealing.

He's the luckiest kid in the world.

He's got $500,000.

That night at the table, my seat gets hot. I win another two million. That's the way it goes. When you really don't need it, you just keep winning.

I call C.L. and inform her answering machine (she will not pick up) that I am sending her $100,000. I ask her to forgive me.

She does not call to say thanks. She does cash the check.

What I Know about the Rain

58.

What I know about the rain is that when it falls, there's like a million drops of water per second. The grass gets wet, so does the sand.

What I know about money is that a million dollars isn't a lot.

The poor say, I wish I had a million dollars. Why do they say that? The poor will have a million dollars. Over their lifetime. Twenty-five thousand dollars a year times 40 years of working, say driving a bus (not counting raises, not counting promotions, not counting overtime and second jobs), equals one million dollars. So you will have your million, but it is not a lot.

I see a million dollars at my private Hold'em table every night stacked up in chips. One night I won a million. One night I won two millions. One night I lost three millions. Don't get excited. It's just three millions sitting side by side, and a million isn't much.

I hear the regular people say, Honey, what are we going to do? We just lost our last $500. They're going to kick us out of our room. How are we going to get back to Peoria?

They've got suitcases full of touristy T-shirts and children with nice haircuts and a bunch of glossies signed by Wayne Newton, but waiting outside for them is a car with no gas. They've got a wallet full of charge cards that won't charge anymore. They're on the verge of divorce. Their little church picnic, it seems, got detoured into Sin City.

It's not even pocket change for me. It can make or break them. Five hundred dollars.

How many drops of rain is that?

What I know about the rain is that it falls on the just and the unjust. But sometimes the just, and their brood of tow-headed children, can't catch 500 drops to get back home. Me, now, if I took a mind to it, I could put a dollar on every drop of rain that falls for a second. For 15 seconds, at least. That's today. Last month, I could do it for a whole half-minute. A million dollars a second for 30 seconds.

Yeah, I play with the big boys. I *am* one of the big boys. In Vegas, I'm what they call a whale. When I place a bet, it can break the house. When I place a bet, they call upstairs to the big boss to ask for permission. When I place a bet, everyone holds their breath.

". . . and I used to be a school bus driver. Yup. Got a few minutes one day, I'll tell you my story. I'm nobody's judge, but why bring children to this hell, Daddy? Kids. God bless 'em. Here's 500 bucks—here's 1,000 bucks. Take it. No, don't thank me. It's just rain," I tell him. "Rain. Whales are awash in rain. You heard me right. Now get your ass back to Peoria. Have a nice day."

The rain hardly ever falls in Las Vegas, but today it is coming down. There are people outside just looking at it fall. I am one of them. It reminds me of Miami, where it rains a lot, especially in May. When we were kids, it seemed it rained every day after school in May. You could set the clock to it. Two-thirty, the school bell rings. Two-thirty-one, here comes the rain. Afternoon showers. Girls hated it. Boys loved it. We would take off our shoes and splash in the puddles all the way home. Throw mud balls at the girls and their colorful umbrellas.

There's another gambler out there looking at the rain. He's about my age. Well-dressed. Wearing one of those cowboy ties that look like a shoestring, what they call a bolo. His body is tanned and lean. A lifetime chain smoker, he's puffing thoughtfully on a cigarette. He's a good Hold'em player. I've never gotten the best of him, though he's gotten the best of me once or twice. I don't hold a grudge. Let's call him U.

U is one of the big boys, too. U is a whale.

He was born on the family farm in Wisconsin. A dairy farm. He was the middle child of seven, all girls except for him. All lanky, big-boned, fair-eyed farm folk were U and his female siblings. All aching to do anything in life but go into the family business.

His older sisters married well, and early; the younger ones, who are still single and in their 30s, are more into collecting college degrees than husbands. One heads an architectural firm. One, the scientist, is a top technology consultant. The baby of the family, the psychiatrist, is a college professor and writer of several very popular books on depression. She was on *Oprah* twice.

I once asked U if he was jealous of his sisters' success. He answered, "Can't say that I am. They're my sisters and I'm proud of them. Besides, with the kind of money I make doing this . . . it's kind of embarrassing, but I'd bet you I'm richer than all of them put together. Ha-ha. They should put *me* on *Oprah*."

U hated school, so he ran away from home at 16, lied about his age, and joined the army. He wanted to see the world. He wanted to learn about life. What he saw was Asia. Japan. Korea. The Philippines. Thailand. What he learned was how to gamble.

"I used to go to this gambling house in Manila every time I got leave. There was this woman there who was kind of a local celebrity with the cards. I used to like to play against her, though she usually cleaned me out. Heck, it was good just watching her play. She knew every angle. She knew all the tricks. Man, this girl knew her poker. I tell you, she could play the game without even looking at her cards and clean out most men I know. You don't expect a woman to be that good with the cards, and she wasn't cheating either. She wasn't the best-looking thing in the world, and she was almost as old as my mother, but I spent some quality time with her, if you know what I mean. It was worth it, too. Cards wasn't the only thing she taught me."

When the army finally spit U out, he was 30 years old and ready to go high stakes. His father, still sore at him for sneaking off, was twisting his arm to take over the farm, which was not what U had in mind at all. But he made a deal with himself (and his father). He would give it a year trying to earn his living as a gambler, and if he failed he would make his father happy and take over the farm.

Six months later, U had banked his first million. Two years later, he had won his second World Championship of Poker tournament.

"Two in a row. Yeah, that's me. My Filipina honey taught me real good. The funny thing is, I'm not like most gamblers. I've never had what you would call bad luck. The cards seem to always fall my way. And when the cards aren't working, I make my own luck—I bluff and win. In some ways, I'm not a gambler at all. Not like you . . . and some of the rest. For me it's all business. I feel like I'm a corporation, you know? It's all business. I got a job to do, I go in and I do it. I take no pleasure in it at all. I mean, I've been doing this going on ten years and I've never been broke, never been through a down time, never had a bad run of luck, never come close to going back to the farm."

"What ever happened to it?"

"My big sister and her husband, the doctor, took it over, then sold it first chance they got after my daddy was in the ground. I don't think he ever forgave me for that. But I'm no farmer. That life's way too hard. I hated it."

"You like gambling, though?"

"I hate this, too," he says. "Poker has to be the most boring game in the world. You sit there hour after hour after hour, throwing away shitty hands, waiting for a good draw, only to get your ass beat on the river by some chaser. Maybe that's why I'm so good at it. I hate it. It bores me. I'd rather be fishing. I'd rather be on the farm, ha-ha. I'm just here for the money."

Today U sees me leaning up against the wall, sheltered from the rain under the valet parking canopy, and he strolls over. He gestures with his eyes, Want a cigarette? I accept one from him, though I am trying to quit again. He goes to light it for me, but I tuck it behind my ear. He smiles and assumes my pose next to me—butt propped against the wall, left knee slightly bent. Two successful gamblers, enjoying a quiet moment outside, watching the rain. One in bolo tie. One in black cowboy hat. Between the two, there's got to be 30 million dollars. Last month it would have been closer to 50 million, but I've had a bad streak. I lost my focus a little bit. The good players could read me like a book. See, try as I might, I'm not like U. For me it's not a business. I still like the rush too much. I still do it for the rush. Not the money. I have lots of money now. Thank God.

U says, "Remember that girl I was with?"

I nod.

"Well, that's over. She says I can't be trusted. She says I'm a cheap bastard. She says I'm a liar."

We are side by side, looking off in the same direction. If I glance to my right, I can see his profile. Watch his jaw muscles as he talks. His muscles don't move much, which helps him in poker. U gives off no signs. No *tells*, as we call them. U is a stone face. All the good ones are like this. They've got a tough face to read. Me, I'm just lucky.

"What got to me," he says, "is the lie part. Calling me a liar. I made a promise when I met her that I would not lie. I laid all my cards on the table. This is who I am. This is what I do. This is what you are going to have to deal with. She said, Okay, I can live with that."

I chuckle. "But she couldn't, right?"

"She couldn't," he says. "And somehow this is supposed to be my fault. So now she's moving out. She's taking all of her shit. All of the shit I bought her. I'm trying to talk to her, see if maybe we can work it out, but she gets this restraining order from the court telling me I'm not supposed to even be there, at my own house, when she packs up her shit. And probably some of my shit, too."

"She would steal from you?"

"I don't know," U says. "No. I don't think so. She's not that kind of girl. This girl was solid, man."

"She was pretty. You guys made a nice couple."

"She says I'm sick."

"We're all sick."

"She says I need help."

"We all need help."

"Not me."

"Yes, you too, U. Even you, U."

His cigarette is squeezed between his fingers. Suddenly he waves it in the air like a wand. "Not me," U says, waving his magic cigarette. "I don't buy into that crap. There's no such thing as addiction."

"There is addiction, my friend, and we are it. We're like alcoholics. We're like dope fiends. We're like sex addicts. We get horny for the gamble."

His magic wand waves. "There is no addiction. It's all a lie made up by the tight-asses in our society and supported by a dangerous religious cult called Anonymous. Alcoholics Anonymous. Gamblers Anonymous. Bullshit. You gamble. You drink. You don't want to gamble anymore? Then stop. You don't want to drink anymore? Then stop. It's not about 12 steps. It's about willpower. It's about free will. God can't save you if you don't want to be saved. Free will is a bitch. Deal with it."

"It's a sickness. I got that monkey on my back. I'm preaching the monkey's gospel. I'm the devil's evangelist. I'm sick, U. You too, U."

I'm grinning.

U is not.

I've had this argument before with U. I love baiting U. Plus, it might help him get his mind off his girl.

Swelling up, U pushes that magic cigarette wand between his teeth and clenches hard, momentarily losing his stone face, grumbling, "No one says an athlete is addicted to the game! He throws all day and all night until he gets that curveball right. He does this for 25 or 30 years—even when there is no game. He does it so long and so hard, one arm grows longer than the other, but that's not addiction. That's called athletic perfection. Mastery of craft. He gets to go to the Hall of Fame. What it is, P, is your basic tight-asses don't approve of gambling. Your basic tight-asses don't approve of drinking. Your basic tight-asses don't approve of dope smoking, so they call it a vice, a crime, a sin, and now a damn sickness. Is a baseball player addicted to baseball? Is a chess master addicted to chess?"

"That sounds fine and all, but I don't know too many chess players with withdrawal symptoms when they can't play chess. Sneaking out of the house to play chess?"

"That's not the point."

"Well, what *is* the point? A baseball player is losing his house *because* he throws too much? They tell him to stop throwing or he's gonna lose his house? I'm not following this one, bro. I'm telling you, there's a devil with a pitchfork behind it all, and on the other side is a loving God telling your ass to get out of the casino forever."

"That's just silly. Gambling is a game. A *game*. You want to stop, then stop. Keep me away from your goddamn 12 steps. Keep me away from your goddamn false religion."

"I can't seem to get past even the first step myself."

"You shouldn't have to. Just quit if you want to quit. Free will."

"Is that right?" I say to him.

"That is right."

"She ain't coming back, is she?"

"Oh man! Shit, shit, shit." Now he's shaking his head. Looks like he's fighting back tears, or maybe something stronger. Maybe I went too far. "Nah. Guess not. Nah, she ain't coming back," he says hoarsely. His cigarette has been smoked down to a stub. He takes one last drag, then flicks it to the ground and mashes out the glow with his spit-shined cowboy heel. The rain stops falling. He says in a stronger voice, "It's just pussy, man."

I tip my hat. "Yeah."

He says to me, "What about that girl *you* were with?"

I don't want to talk about C.L. Too hard. I say to U, "Are you in that tournament tonight?"

"Naw, I'm gonna play the tables. Make more money at the tables tonight."

"I like the tournaments tonight."

"I like the tables."

"Just making money."

"Just making money, baby," U retorts with a dry laugh.

"You know it, brother," I tell him, dry-laughing back.

U extends his hand. I slap him five. He slaps me five back and walks away. All in all, he's a real cool white boy. A real cool gambler. A true professional. He's all business again. There are no tells in his walk. From his walk, you wouldn't know whether it was raining or the sun was shining. Whether it was Vegas or Miami. Whether it was the desert or the beach.

I can't tell, good as I am.

THE MONKEY'S GOSPEL

59.

(It Is a Gun. It Is a Gun.)

There are only two kinds of gamblers: the lucky and the broke.

I *am* the lucky kind.

I own three homes, which I do not live in. I lease them out to movie stars. I own two cars—two very nice cars—both of which I drive.

Depending on what day of the month it is, I am invested in 50 to 100 businesses. I have stocks and bonds worth seven million dollars on today's market. I also have, much to the dismay of my accountant, seven million dollars in cash in the bank, of all places. We have argued over this many times, but I like to have easy access to it, an easy access that I hope never to use. I just like to know that if I ever wanted to, I could cash a check for seven million dollars. My poor accountant. He worries about me.

Reckless. Wasteful. Bad money management, he calls it, but I know what he is really thinking: What if you get the itch again?

He sees how I live my life, he sees where I live, and he does not trust. He keeps waiting for the inevitable slide back. For me to cash the whole thing in and bet it all on black. There is always that possibility, I guess. You might say I'm sort of high risk.

I live in these casinos. I wouldn't live anywhere else. I live with a deck of cards in my pocket. But I do not gamble. When I am not downstairs watching the others, I play solitaire in my room. I play solitaire seven or eight hours a day. It helps. It scratches the itch.

I should be happy. I think I am. I am rich. I am near what I love. The monkey is off my back. What makes me happiest, though, is knowing that I have lost everything I own four or five times over and I still have all this. This is a lot. This didn't used to be a lot. This used to be what you start with in order to get more.

Bet these little millions, bet these little chips, I would tell myself, and then you will be rich. That is how I used to think.

See, you get in this zone where you're risking your entire net worth every day and every night and the rush is so incredible. These $100,000-ante games, with these captains of industry and famous athletes, these money men, these really rich guys, these whales, this pot with two million in it, and you raise it four million, and these big shots fold their cards—these really big shots fold—and you rake in another couple million. They deal you another hand, and you look in the hole, and I'll be damned if it's not aces again. But something goes wrong this time—or maybe it goes right.

You say, Aces, aha, I can win another big pot. I can be rich. I can bet everything I'm worth on this hand and be rich. And you look down at your chips—you've got like 10 million dollars in chips sitting in front of you. You multiply that by the number of big shots sitting at the table who you figure will call the hand—they call every hand, these three chasers. One of them, the Chinese guy, he owns all the shoelace factories in Taiwan. He's always joking, If I lose 10 or 20 million dollars while I'm here in Vegas, no problem. I just go back home and raise the worldwide price of shoelaces by a penny, ha-ha-ha-ha-ha-ha.

It's kind of funny. It's kind of not. He's got money to throw away, he's a whale, he's a whale so big he makes you look like a guppy—but you've got aces. You can clean him out. You can send him back to Taiwan cleaned out. Raise the price of shoelaces worldwide, ha-ha-ha-ha-ha-ha. Then you will be worth . . . but you are already worth . . . There's 10 million in chips sitting in front of you!

This is when you say to yourself, But it's only luck. You are not magic. You are not special. You have no great skill. It's only luck. Ten million is ten million. Ten million is a lot. Ten million is too much and aces can be beat. You know from personal experience that aces get beat all the time. If he beats these aces, he takes your 10 million, and the price of shoelaces won't be affected at all.

Ha-ha-ha-ha-ha-ha.

But you will go back to driving a bus.

Ha-ha-ha-ha-ha-ha. Ha-ha-ha-ha-ha-ha. Ha-ha-ha-ha-ha-ha.

This is when you freak.

Simply put, you freak out. You've got aces and you freak out. You lay your cards down. You fold your aces. You are freaking out.

You watch the rest of the hand play out. The three chasers are in it to the end. The Chinese guy from Taiwan wins the pot. A big pot.

You know how much it had in it? Twenty million dollars.

You know what he won it with? Two jacks.

You would have killed him. You would have cleaned him out. What the hell did you fold your aces for? They were aces!

You rack up your chips and cash out. You leave the table. You go upstairs and lie on your bed. You are alone. You hear a heart pounding fast. You hear sobbing. You reach for the phone and dial the one that you love, and you tell her, I just blew 20 million dollars.

She says, You lost 20 million dollars?

You say, No. I blew it. I folded. I should have stayed in the hand. I would have won.

She says, So why did you fold?

You say, Because . . .

She says, Because what?

Because . . . I don't know.

You don't know?

I don't know. I don't know.

And she says, Maybe you should find a new line of work.

You don't know. You don't know. You don't know. So all week you are grieving. The monkey is preaching his obscene gospel. All week you're losing like crazy. It's seven days before you win another hand. The money is going away. You're too ashamed to count how much per day. So you stop for a test. A teensy-weensy little test. Just to see what it feels like to spend a month at the beach doing nothing.

Suddenly, it's like a weight lifted off your shoulders.

Well, not suddenly, because the first few days are hard. The nights harder. It helps if there is a woman there with you, and there always is because you have plenty of money to flash. This pretty island girl, she strokes your ego in a way that almost fills the void. And you think, Here, now. There is this. This is nice. Maybe not as good as gambling, but nice.

A month later you go to your money, and it has grown. That is the day you realize that you are rich. You have had millions of dollars before this, but this is the first day you realize that you are truly rich.

You are at a beach on an island. You are the rich guy. All the girls are after you. You let them catch you. This feels sort of good. You go to your bank account, and again it has grown, and you think, Did I really lose three million dollars in one night?

It is a crazy idea: If you leave your money alone, it will be there for you the next day. If you do not gamble . . . shit, your bills are too small to eat through this mint, so where is the money going to go?

The monkey interjects a cynical thought: What good is having all that money if you don't use it?

You tell the monkey to screw off. Beat it!

He digs his claws in deep, so deep you can't breathe, and you are pleading, pleading, Leave me alone, please, please, please leave me alone, oh my God, don't kill me, you're killing me, monkey—and you grab that pretty island girl and you fuck her and you fuck her until she swears you love her. Then you fuck her sister, too.

You end your vacation. You go back home to Vegas, but you continue the test. You play your solitaire. You live in your casino. You chase your pretty girls. You do not gamble. It is hard, but you do not gamble. The desire is still there. So is your money, and it is growing—larger now than even your desire.

You think: So that's what banks do, they pay you to hold your money. What a concept. Did I really lose three million dollars in one night? What was I thinking? Oh my God.

The monkey says, You also won 10 million dollars in one night, don't forget.

But you are learning to ignore the monkey, who does not have one single original thought in his head.

Then you see someone hit a jackpot, and the monkey digs back in deep. The itch wants to be scratched. So you scratch. You and that woman, what was her name? Now, *she* was a degenerate. You scratch that itch, man. You scratch. Half a million dollars in 12 hours. Every penny of it feels like blood. The monkey is humming sweet songs. He is happy to be back. And that woman, what was her name? She wants to keep going, she says she has a hunch about the end machine—so you let her keep going. A hundred dollars a pop. Then four machines at a time—her purse on one, her drink on another, her cigarettes on another, her lighter on the lucky end machine. Four hundred dollars a pop. Another two hundred thousand down. The jackpot goes off, finally, and damn if she doesn't win it. Eight hundred thousand dollars! And she's hugging you and squeezing you and then (upstairs) blowing you (*ping! ping!*), and you're thinking, But didn't we pump $700,000 into those things? That's only $100,000 net profit. Didn't I earn more than that in interest while chilling down on that island with that girl?

Good questions. Good questions all. Monkey, any thoughts?

So you play your solitaire while that woman (what was her name? what was her husband's name?) takes her winnings back downstairs to the machines, and you plan another test: If she wins again, then you will gamble, but if she comes back up here a week from now asking for money—

Of course, in a week she has given it all back.

All of it.

Less than a week.

Eight *hundred thousand* dollars.

You say, Amazing.

The monkey says, But that's not the point—she's a degenerate. It won't happen to you, I promise.

And she says, Can I have some more money?

You give her $1,000, this woman who is now used to playing it $400 a pop, and she slaps you, shrieking, This is all you give me?

It gets so bad, you have to call security to your room.

Amazing, you say.

The test continues. And the itch. And the solitaire. A daily diet of solitaire. God, do you need your solitaire.

You go three months without gambling, without thinking about your bank account, but when you finally check it, the money has grown some more.

You figure it in your head: The interest is more than a year's worth of really big jackpots. And you do not smell like smoke. Your eyes are not heavy with sleep. Your bills are paid.

But that girl (S, her name was S), she comes back to you. She says that she is leaving her husband, her children, for you. She says that she loves only you. But you know better. You say to her, No one is putting a gun to your head. You don't have to keep playing. You can quit. Your life will improve. Believe me, I know. She says, But I can't. You say, Nobody has a gun to your head. She says, It is a gun. It is a gun. It is right here against my head. You say, You got that monkey on your back, is what. You're preaching the monkey's gospel. She says, Man, this is so much bullshit. I want to be with you, don't you fucking understand? You tell her, But I have someone already. She says, No you don't, you degenerate. Stop fucking with my head, okay? You don't have anybody. Everybody knows that. You tell her, I have somebody, I really do, somebody who I love. Somebody whose love is strong enough to make me see that there is no gun to my head. Somebody whose love is bigger than this thing. Somebody whose love I miss. She says, Not me. No way. I don't love anybody that much. Shit. I just want to gamble. You tell her, Thank you for being honest at least. Then you open your safe and your heart and give her a hundred thousand. She takes it like she's in a hurry. She forgets to kiss you. A *hundred* thousand. *No* kiss. You call the one whose love has saved you.

You tell her, I love you. I want you back. I'm not that man anymore. I beat it. I finally got that monkey off my back. I want to come home.

You hear the tears in her voice when the one you love tells you,

There's no home here for you to come home to. I've found somebody else.

She hangs up without waiting to hear what you will say.

You can't believe it. You simply can't believe it's been that long. Four and a half years have passed since you've lived at home. Six months since you've visited.

Too late.

You call the other one, the one who had it so bad you had to let her go, had to kick her to the curb for her own good. You tell her you are desperately lonely. You tell her you are thinking dark thoughts. You tell her about the monkey. You tell her you think you want to die. C.L. tells you, Send me the money. I'll be there on the next plane.

You tell her, No money. I'll send you the ticket.

She insists, Cash. I've got to clear up some things down here.

No cash, you insist.

She says, I've got to clear up some things down here. Plus, I need to buy some new clothes. I want to look good for you, my love. Send me the cash. Load the card. Stop treating me like a child.

You tell her, We're talking about dying here. I'm telling you I'm going to kill myself, do you hear? This is me. This is me!

Her voice is calm, controlled, carefully masking the desperation, which almost, almost, almost doesn't come through. She says: I need the cash. Load the card with cash and I'll be there for you. I still love you. I swear.

This is what she says, but what you hear behind her speaks a louder truth. You hear them. You hear the machines behind her. It is the diamond machine. She is there right now, banging the diamond machines in the casino in the swamp. You know what will happen if you load her card with cash. There is nothing that can tear her away from that machine when she's like this. Whether you send her that cash or not, she will not get on a plane and leave a hot machine behind. Whether you kill yourself or not, you will never see her again. You know all this and yet you load her card with cash (three grand, a teensy-weensy test). You still have hope.

You call back 15 minutes later and she doesn't pick up.

Twenty minutes later, you call the bank and check the balance on the card, and she has withdrawn every penny you sent.

What did you expect?

But you own three fabulous homes and two very nice cars, the monkey reminds.

He's back.

With claws and teeth.

You run.

You get in one of those nice cars and you drive. Three hours later you stop driving. You do not know where you are. There is sand and sky on either side of the road. You get out and look at the desert. It is desolate and it is beautiful. It is not Miami. It is not home. But it is beautiful. All that sand. Cars hardly ever pass, but a car pulls up. Before you decide that it is the same white station wagon you've been seeing in your rearview mirror all afternoon, a short, stocky man with a very red face jumps out of it and hurtles into you, knocking you to the ground. You recover. Now the two of you are wrestling on the hot road. He is crazy. He says he wants to kill you with his bare hands. He's got his bare hands around your throat. You hear children crying, and you think of your own boys, whom you haven't been to see in almost six months. Has it been that long? But you have houses and cars and money and a monkey and this guy is strangling you. You reach up and put your thumbs in the man's eyes. He growls and adds more muscle to the death grip on your neck. You strain with all your might and head-butt him. Push him off. Spring up. Lunge to your car, grasp at the door. You hear his agonized groan behind you. You hear him say, Stop, fucker, or I'm gonna shoot you. You turn, and there is a gun in his hand. You raise your hands and say, But why? What do you want? He says, Fucker. Oh, you fucker. He's rubbing his eyes with his fist. He's got the gun aimed at your heart. He's saying, S is my wife.

He pulls the trigger.

What you remember best is the sudden thunder, drowning out the cries of the children, and the blow is like a sledgehammer to your chest, slamming you back against your nice car, and you collapse to your knees. You remember being on your knees. You remember trying to pray. Trying to clasp your hands. Trying to pray to Him who died for all your sins, trying to tell Him:

pleaseGodpleaseIpromiseGodpleaseIpromiseI . . .

You hear the crying of children again, and you see their red faces leaning out of the windows of the station wagon. They are crying, Daddy, no, Daddy, no, Daddy, no.

S's husband backs up. He looks down at the gun in his hand. He looks down at you. At your red blood on the ground same color as the blood pouring out of his nose. His children screaming behind him. He's sobbing into his cell phone, I just shot somebody. We need an ambulance. I shot him bad.

Again there is the sound of thunder. A gentle rain begins to fall in the desert. Against your face. The screaming of children. They are the children on the bus. Quiet down, children. Quiet down.

pleaseGodpleaseIpromiseGodpleaseI

Quiet down.

You black out.

Grace That Is Greater Than All Our Sin

60.

He should have aimed for my ass instead of my heart. A gambler is more asshole than heart.

But you made it. You survived.

Just lucky, is all. I am a lucky-ass gambler.

You are Roy Orbison, too.

I like to wear black.

And the cowboy hat?

I like the cowboy hat because when I walk into a casino, people know it's me. They see the hat. They say, There goes P. There goes the bus driver. I like the hat. But I do it mostly for the fans. It's kind of a costume.

You wore the hat when you drove a school bus?

No. The hat is new. The hat is cool. The rings are cool, too. Check out my bling-bling.

Indeed, you are among the sharpest dressers in Vegas. So is your lady friend this evening.

Yeah. She sure knows how to wear a gown.

The black cowboy hat and a beautiful woman in a low-cut gown on your arm. That's how they know it's you.

She is beautiful.

A different woman every night.

Yes, well, you know how it is. But this one tonight is different.

Is it a love thing?

I won't go that far. I don't know. Maybe. We've known each other for most of our lives. We split up for a while due to life circumstances, but it's kind of working out for us now. I met her in fourth grade, you know?

Is that so?

I swear to God. We sat next to each other, but I couldn't talk to her. She was so beautiful. I sat next to her for like a whole year. The only thing I ever said to her was, You dropped your pencil. Then the next year, we sat next to each other again, and this time I told her, That's a pretty dress. In sixth grade, it was her who talked to me. She said, Do you like me or not? Just like that. I said, Yes. And she kissed me on the nose. Craziest thing. That made us kind of like boyfriend and girlfriend. Then we went to different junior and senior high schools. I met people. She met people. I met this dingbat and got her pregnant. Life went on. Then we bumped into each other again. And like *blam*—we got married and had kids. Life was perfect.

So she's your wife?

Ah, no.

But you said you got married.

She's just a friend. Comes to see me sometimes. When I was recovering after that guy shot me . . . She came and nursed me back to health.

Huh? I thought you said— Well, anyway, I hear you're quite the ladies' man. There are so many stories about you. Women. Violence.

Hmmm. No comment.

You are in the World Championship of Poker. You are at the final table. There's only five players left. You are the chip leader.

All that means nothing unless you win it. I am a decent enough poker player. I should win it. It would be nice. But there are other good players at the table.

How does one get to be so good? What is the key to your success? You came out of nowhere.

Nowhere, huh? Well, for me, it's all that I do. I do not play any other card game. I do not play the lottery. I do not play the machines. I do not play any of that one-in-a-million crap. The house has it fixed so you can't win. Only the house wins in those games. At this game, you can win because it's man against man. All of my money comes from this game right here. See, I am very good because my life depends on it. The life of my children. I'm good at poker because I respect it, too. I know what it can do. I've been there. Gambling scares me. I know what it can do.

But it is kind of a glamorous life. You live in a five-star hotel. You hobnob with celebrities. You're a high roller. You've got lots of money.

You know what's special about me? I know exactly how much money I am worth right now.

So do I. I know what I'm worth.

Not like a gambler. A gambler always knows *exactly* how much he's worth. It's always in your head. It's like your wallet is in your head. It can be very exhausting. You know that you have $1,000 in the bank. You know that you just spent $650. You know that your ATM fees are $42.50. You know that your bank fees are $72. You know that the cable, water, and phone are asking for $305. You know that you are short. You know that you have to go back into the casino and find at least $69.50 to keep everything going. Or you can stall the cable and the phone, but not the water—your wife will definitely notice the water missing, and you cannot tell her that you have gambled it away. Oh, no, no, no, no, no, you cannot do that. So you go back into the casino and lose another hundred. Now you have no choice but to borrow. Your sister lends you $200. Again. Now, after you have paid everything, you will have $30.50, which will not get you to your next payday after gas and groceries, so what the heck good is $30.50? You can go back into the casino and try to turn it into something bigger. And you do. You turn that $30.50 into $400. Now you can breathe. Now you have paid your bills, and, not counting what you owe your sister, you are worth $400, which is exactly what is in your wallet and in your head. You can breathe. Or you can go back into the casino with every cent you own in the world, $400, since every cent you own in the world is already in your wallet. See? How many people do you know who regularly have more in their wallet than in their bank account? When I was worth 20 million dollars, there were days when I had 20 million dollars in chips on the table in front of me. When I was worth $400, same thing. See what I'm saying? So you are worth $400, and if you can increase it to $1,000, your sense of self-worth goes up too. If you can hit a jackpot and increase it to $5,000, your self-worth soars to the sky. Imagine that. In two months of working at a regular job, you can earn $5,000 easy and it feels like nothing to you, but if you risk everything in the world you own, invest 10 or 15 grand, and you get back $5,000, your self-worth soars. But you've just invested 10 or 15 grand to make five and you're happy?

And yet it's different for you. You've got money.

Has to be 50 million dollars passed through my hands over the years at the tables. Maybe 100 million. Where is it? My wife, my ex-wife, the woman in the gown tonight, she thinks the money is cursed. Maybe she's right. It's evil money. The devil's money.

But you're successful.

I invested my whole life. My whole family. And what did I get back? A hotel room and a bank vault full of poker chips.

The presidential suite of a five-star hotel. A bank vault full of *money*.

It's still just a hotel room, not a home. And they're still just poker chips, the wallet in my head says. Six million eight hundred thousand six hundred and twenty-two dollars worth of poker chips.

That's a lot of money.

Last month it was close to 12 million. I had a real bad couple of weeks. I was patient. I played only the strongest hands, but still I got beat. That's why I need to do well in this tournament.

But it's still a lot of money.

It's just chips as long as I can count them. As long as I can count them, I can still play with them. I can still put them on the table. I can still risk them. Why can't I invest that money instead? Why can't I do something safe with it so that it gets out of my head? Why can't I? This is what my accountant wants to know. It's my gambling money, see? And gambling money has only one purpose—to be gambled. It will increase, it will decrease, but it will always be in play as long as it is in my head . . . Right now, I am good. Right now, I am strong. But I don't know how much longer I can resist withdrawing all the chips and dumping the whole bunch of them on black just to see what would happen. Every single day I walk past that roulette wheel. Do you know how much money I would make if I hit? I would be back up close to 12 million. I would be rich.

You are rich.

I'm not rich. All I got is chips.

You are rich, and from what I've seen, you are the most disciplined gambler who ever lived. You do not make a bad bet. That is the secret to your success. You are patient. You wait them out. You manage your chips. You do not chase. You wait until the cards come to you. That's why you are at the final table. That's why you are the chip leader. That's why you are rich. You should write a book. I'd buy it. We all would.

Thanks for that, my friend. Am I all that? Nah, I don't think so. Wow. But it's just luck, really. All I am is lucky. And I'm not rich. I'm just a bus driver in a cowboy hat, is all. But tonight, whether I win or lose in this final round, I don't care, I'm going back afterward to my hotel room to sleep with my wife.

I thought you said she's your ex-wife.

True. But as long as she's in my head, she's just like the chips. She's still in play. I still got a chance. Her fiancé can kiss my ass. Well, sorry, I gotta go. I gotta get back to the table. They're calling me.

Not a problem, thank you for your time. This was great. Just great. Well, ladies and gentlemen, you heard the man himself, the man in the black hat, the one they call the bus driver, our current chip leader, P. The odds-on favorite to win the whole darned thing. He's one of the nicest guys here, and his humility, you gotta admit, is as great as his skill. But despite everything he says, folks, I'd trade my little old life for his any day.

PART III
Man in the Black Hat

How is individual transformation to be achieved? There are some bad habits among individuals such as smoking, drinking liquor, meat eating, and gambling. These bad habits not only degrade the individuals but also inflict hardships on their families. These bad habits have to be given up for the individual to manifest his inherent goodness.

—Sri Sathya Sai Baba

61.

Missy would not say that she was addicted. Not exactly.

An addict looks shady. An addict dresses in shabby clothes and has a tattoo. An addict hangs out with a tough crowd. An addict lives in a real gambling place like Las Vegas or Atlantic City, not sunny Miami.

An addict does not wear Prada.

An addict does not have a purse full of platinum cards, an Ivy League brain, and a supermodel's face and body.

At least she used to have a supermodel's body, back in her 20s and 30s.

But two children, dedication to her career as an executive editor at a publishing house, and a difficult divorce had limited the time she could spend at the gym. In truth, the long hours at her favorite South Florida Indian casino had limited the time she could spend at the gym. So she had put on thirty or so pounds, but it didn't look too bad on her, and her face still looked good.

For forty.

No, Missy was certain that she was not an addict. She found that gambling (small-stakes gambling, such as they had in South Florida) relaxed her. The steady *ping-ping* of the machines was soothing. The frantic up-and-down turns of fortune got her mind off the stresses of work and being a single mother. But lately she found herself spending more and more time at the casino. She found herself frustrated by her cell phone, which seemed to almost always go off just when her machine got hot, or when her machine had gone cold and she was in deep contemplation about which hot numbers to switch to. The calls from the office were a nuisance that could be handled later. The calls from the kids, however, were now being handled with:

"I'm at the office. I'll call you back later."

Or, "Can't you kids take care of it yourself? I'm in an important meeting."

Or, "I'll be there in an hour. I'm stuck in traffic."

—and her hand shielding the mouthpiece from the *ping-ping*.

Money, for the first time in her life, was becoming a problem. Not only was she beginning to have trouble paying her regular bills, but whenever something broke and needed repair or her ailing parents, whom she supported financially, called on her, she found herself stalling for time or getting creative to come up with the funds. She would borrow from her ex-husband and say it was for the kids—the boy, 15, needed sports equipment, the girl, 13, needed strings for her violin. Or she would liquidate a stock. Or she would apply for more credit, which always came because she had a stellar credit record.

Four weeks ago, the bottom seemed to fall out.

A heavy tropical storm had blown through South Florida and torn off a small part of the roof of her four-bedroom Coral Gables home. It was a minor patch job. The deductible was $3,000, but the repair itself was only $2,000. Missy could not come up with the money. She could not believe it. She was maxed out on everything. She had to choose between borrowing from her ex again or applying for more credit. She did both.

The cost of her ex's gift/loan was her spending the night with him in his old bed. She woke up feeling sad and used, and then had to deal with the children, who were already beginning to show signs of having happy fantasies about a reunion of their parents. She felt so low and so depressed that after her ex left, she called in sick and went straight to the casino and blew every penny that he had given/loaned her.

Fortunately, the additional credit came two days later, the roof was repaired, and a few hundred was left over—all of which went to the casino, too.

But then with fifty cents that she scrounged up from the ashtray in the car, she won $10,000. See?

That was four weeks ago. Now Missy was seated at the machine again and down to the last $100 from that $10,000 that she had won, ignoring her ringing phone (the children again) and trying to convince herself that she was not addicted to gambling. She watched, helplessly, as her total went from $100 to $20. She kept pushing the PLAY button. The machine was not hitting anything. Now it was down to $5. When it got down to $1, she said to the black man in the big black cowboy hat sitting but not playing at the machine next to hers, "Can you watch it for me while I go to the ATM?"

This was not desperation, Missy convinced herself. She had a good job. Tomorrow was payday. The money she had blown had been won anyhow, so it was not like she was spending her own money. She was spending their money. The money she was about to withdraw, now that was *her* money, so she would be more cautious with it because she was not addicted to gambling. She was just having a good time. She was just relaxing. Her cell phone went off—the kids again. *So annoying.* Missy cursed and turned it off without answering it.

The black man in the cowboy hat said, "I'll do you one better. I'll give your machine good luck. Would you like that?"

Missy smiled at him politely but shrank away.

You had to be real careful in a casino. The black man was about her age, maybe a few years older. He was of medium height, well-dressed, clean, and not bad-looking. She had seen him in here before. The other gamblers all seemed to know him and like him. She decided he was safe and took his hand. His head bowed and he kissed her on the back of the hand. When he lifted his head again, he tipped his cowboy hat and said, "You go to that ATM, and when you come back I will make your machine lucky for you."

When she came back, he was still there guarding the dollar she had left in her machine. She sat down and he said, "Wait a minute." He put both his hands on top of the machine and brought his lips to the screen and kissed it. "Now it's ready," he said. "Whatever money you lost today it's gonna give back. I guarantee it, or I'll give it to you myself."

Missy muttered glumly, "I lost a lot today."

"How much?"

"With this last $100 I just withdrew?" She figured it in her head. "I'm down $900."

Her heart thumped with excitement as she watched the black man calmly peel off ten hundred-dollar bills from his billfold and plunk them down on her machine beside the control buttons and her box of Virginia Slims.

He tapped the stack of bills with a finger. "That's a thousand. You don't win, you keep it."

"I can't do that," Missy said, desperate though she was. "I can't take that from you."

He winked. "You won't have to. Your machine is lucky now. Play."

"But I can't—"

"I've gotta go to the bathroom," the black man cut her off, and then disappeared, leaving the money on her machine.

Missy watched him go and said to the blue-haired woman, another familiar face, who sat down in the empty seat beside her, "What should I do? Is he crazy? He left his money here."

The woman said, "Him? He's not crazy. He's very lucky."

"I'm not gonna take some black guy's money."

"If you don't want it, I'll take it."

The blue-haired woman wasn't kidding. She reached for the cash on Missy's machine. Missy stopped her with a faster hand. "He left it for *me!*"

The woman clucked her dentures angrily as she turned away from Missy and got back to the business of playing her own machine.

Missy, who still didn't trust the pissed-off blue-haired woman, kept her hand on the black man's stack of hundreds as she played her machine, which had suddenly gotten hot.

The black man returned about fifteen minutes later. Missy still had her hand on his stack of hundreds. She did not believe that he had actually gone to the bathroom. She figured it was just his way of getting her to trust him and play the machine, which had gotten hot and was now up to $875. The black man patted her on the shoulder. Then left his hand there.

Sometimes the hand moved from her shoulder to the small of her back.

Sometimes it was on the back of her neck. Sometimes it was on the strap of her bra. She wasn't exactly sure how she felt about that hand, but she was no fool. It was a lucky hand. Her machine hit an additional $200 while his hand was on her.

When Missy's total reached $1,100, the black man in the cowboy hat removed his hand from her shoulder and said, "Well, my work here is done," and collected his stack of money and replaced it in his billfold, which, Missy noted, was thick with hundred-dollar bills.

"Thank you," Missy said to him.

"It's gonna lose now," he told her. "You better cash out and go to another machine. All the luck is gone out of this one."

"I think it's hot," said Missy, who did not believe in moving from a hot machine.

"Suit yourself." The black man tipped his hat and vanished into the ocean of people milling about but not playing.

There were many people in the casino tonight. It was crowded, smoke-filled, and loud. *Ping-ping. Ping-ping.* Every now and then Missy would look back to see if he was watching her. She never saw him, but somehow she knew that he was still back there. Her machine went up to $1,200, then down to $800, then up to $1,000, then down to $400, then up to $480, then down to $220. She wanted to get up, cut her losses, but she kept thinking that it would get hot again. It had to. When her machine got down to $43, Missy got up and walked a complete counter-clockwise circle around her seat for luck. She sat back down and her total shot up to $93. It worked! Then it stopped working, and the total plummeted to three dollars. Now she was desperate. She smoked the last three cigarettes in the pack, lighting the new one from the old. She turned to the skinny man who had replaced the blue-haired woman at the machine next to her. "Could you watch this for me while I go to the ATM?"

The skinny man nodded and placed his free hand on her seat. She did not go to the ATM. She made a complete circuit of the casino before she spotted the cowboy hat. He was chatting with a white man in a coat and tie and very shiny shoes. She grabbed his hand. "I need more luck."

"You need help is what you need," he said. He shot a mischievous glance to his friend in the coat and tie and mumbled, "What are we going to do with them, professor?" His friend smiled back and then disappeared into the crowd. The black man said to Missy, "You blew all that money after I told you to get up. Shame on you. You should have gone to another machine. You gamblers never learn."

"I am not a gambler."

He winked. "Neither am I."

"Then what are you?" Maybe she was lying to herself about not being a gambler, but she had seen him in here many times, this black man in the cowboy hat, and she had never seen him play the machines. Maybe he was a poker player who did his gambling in the back rooms. "What are you?" she repeated.

"I am a lucky gambler," the black man said, tipping his hat.

Missy wasn't sure she understood him. Maybe he was crazy, but he was not dangerous and he was lucky and she still had his hand. She had decided that if she could just hit something big today, she would never, ever, ever, ever, ever gamble again. She would get her life together and never come back to this place. She stroked his hand and pouted prettily. "Make my machine lucky again," she pleaded.

The black man took both her hands in his and pulled her close to his body. He said, "I have something better for you."

He thumbed through his billfold until he came to a hundred with a torn corner. He put it in her hand and then pressed her hand against her chest. "This is a lucky hundred. Do not put it in the machine. Put it on your seat. Put other money in the machine, but never put this in the machine."

"What do you mean?"

"I'll show you."

After she made the necessary quick detour to her ATM, he followed her back to her machine. The skinny man was still there with his hand on her seat, but he was standing because he had lost all of his own money. Someone else was sitting at his machine now, but he had stuck around to guard Missy's three dollars. He told her all this as if she owed him something. She said thanks, and the skinny man said, "Whatever," bitterly, and left.

The black man instructed Missy to rest the hundred with the torn corner on her seat and then insert a hundred of her own, which she did.

"What's this supposed to do?"

"This is lucky protection money. It will make sure that you don't lose any money."

"What do you mean?"

"Sit down on this hundred and play," the black man said. "You won't lose. I guarantee it. If you lose, I'll pay you double."

Missy sat down on the hundred and played. For 20 minutes the machine went up and down. Then it got cold and went down to $10. Just as she was beginning to yield to despair, it went back up to $100. Then it went up to $150.

"See?" the black man said. "You will not lose as long as your fine butt is sitting on that hundred. You'll go down, but you will always come back up again."

"But will I win?"

"Not too much. A few bucks, maybe, if you cash out when you're up a little bit. Like right now if you cash out."

"I don't like this kind of luck. This is crap. This is small-time. I need to get back at least the thousand I lost today. I need to win a jackpot, that's what I really need. Kiss the machine like you did before. I want that kind of luck."

The black man said sadly, "Kissing the machine only works once a day. You blew it."

Missy pouted. "Don't you have any other kind of luck?"

"Yes," the man in the cowboy hat said. "Oh yes."

He had his hand on her back. He brought his mouth close to her ear. A hint of Dentyne. A hint of tobacco. "But I don't know if you're ready for that kind of luck yet."

Missy said, "Is it guaranteed to work?"

"Guaranteed."

"Let's do it."

His mouth was in her ear again. "We can't do it here."

"Where can we do it?"

"I have a room upstairs."

Missy gasped, moving her ear away from his mouth. "What are you saying?" she demanded.

"For this luck to work, it's not about kissing machines. The luck has to flow from me into you."

Missy considered this silently. She felt ashamed as she whispered, "Is it guaranteed?"

"My money guarantees it." He took out his billfold. "What's the jackpot up to? $6,800? I got that covered easy."

Missy rose from her seat, sighing. He was not an ugly man, she told herself. She picked up the torn hundred she had sat on and handed it to him. He put it back in his billfold. She reported, "Over the past month, I am down $10,000!"

The black man shrugged, and he, I, said, "I got that covered, too."

Ping. Ping. Ping. Ping. Ping.

62.

Of course, it was a con.

There was no luck imbued in the machine through his kiss. There was no luck in the torn hundred-dollar bill. And there certainly would be no luck flowing from his body into hers in the room upstairs. The only luck this black man had was in the incredible amount of money he possessed, money that he seemed only too glad to hand over once the lucky act had been completed.

Missy had to admit that the act itself was not so bad. He was patient. He was unselfish. He was skillful. No, it was not bad at all, just a bit embarrassing. She finally (gloomily) admitted, "I'm addicted. There's no other way to explain it."

There's no other way to explain that she had called in sick and come here again. No other way to explain that she had been here 18 hours straight. That last week she had spent 48 hours here, not counting the catnaps on a blanket in the parking lot in her car, the little breaks in the action before returning to play again. No other way to explain that she hadn't seen her children today and most of yesterday and had turned off her cell phone so that they could not disturb her play. No other way to explain it. But that was the past. Now there was a glimmer of hope because of this black man.

She had been in his suite for a little over two hours. He was at his desk counting the bills that he had removed from his room safe. Lean and tightly muscled, he was naked except for his cowboy hat. She was naked in his bed under the covers. She had been thoroughly loved by this man and now he was going to pay her $10,000. It would get her back on her feet. She would never gamble again, she knew that. She would not even go downstairs and try the machines some more now that he had given her a lucky fuck, as he had called it. She would take this lucky fuck money and rebuild her life.

He counted out the money for her in ten stacks of ten and left it on the bed. He instructed, "Put it in your pocketbook and get out of here as fast as you can. You don't know who's watching you in this place. Be careful."

He was still naked. Missy decided that she liked him. It was a con, but it was a good con. "Who are you really?" she said. "I'm an editor. Maybe I'll do a book about you. You're weird, but you're interesting. Who are you?"

He grinned. "I am a man in a cowboy hat."

"Who are you really?"

He went over to his desk and picked up a photograph. It was actually a reprint of a cover from *Time* magazine, under the banner, *World Championship of Poker*—he was in it in his cowboy hat with several other players who were probably famous in the gambling world though Missy did not know their names. They were posed around a poker table with the brown, blue, and burgundy chips stacked up by the thousands in front of them. The naked black man held the photograph up to his chest. He put his finger on a place high on his chest that was hairless and bore some kind of scar.

Looking at the photo, Missy thought she understood. "Oh, you're a professional gambler."

"No," he said, still fingering the scar on his chest. "You don't understand. This is a bullet hole, and I got it because of what I am."

"Tell me about it."

"It's time for you to go home now, Missy."

He turned away from her. She got out of the bed and began to dress. He did not look at her while she dressed, but she looked at him. He had taken off the hat. He was wearing a robe now, seated at his desk looking down intently at the photo, fingering the chest wound again.

Missy left his room and went downstairs. The machines called to her, and since she had $10,000 in her bag, she went to them despite her promise never to do it again. She was there for close to an hour. She banged it hard. Harder than she ever had. At $200 a pop. They took $7,000 from her in less than an hour and seemed willing to take more. As she pulled herself away from the machine, she wept great big tears. But she made it away with $3,000 remaining in her purse. She saw the irony of it all: that sleeping with a strange black man for $10,000 was only the second stupidest thing she had ever done. The stupidest thing was giving $7,000 of it back less than an hour later to a machine that went *ping-ping*. She held a napkin to her face as she wept. "My God. My God. What's wrong with me?"

He intercepted her as she passed the casino's café, as she was just about to turn around and give it one more desperate try. He took her in his arms and he held her and he told her, "Go home now. You can do it. Go home. Your children are waiting for you. Your life is waiting for you. Get your life back, Missy. This is not life, this is death."

"But I . . . but I . . ."

"Go home."

And he held her like that and would not let her go until she was able to find her feet and leave. It was the greatest thing anybody had ever done for her. She left and she never returned. He had saved her from becoming a total degenerate—as he was.

PART IV
Penitent

63.

T'hey are not lucky, the old man and the young girl.

In fact, they are very unlucky.

Especially the girl. A tall, slender brown-skinned thing with juicy lips and alluring eyes. She is wearing the kind of skirt that I like. Tight. Short. Showing lots of leg. Flaunting that ghetto booty. Nice. Real nice. I keep right on looking.

The man she is with is a thickset older brother, well over six-three, with dark skin, rough features, and shocking white hair. He is banging the machines at five dollars a pop while the pretty girl coaches: "Change it to the 9s. Yeah. Now put a 6 in it. No, don't change your zero card. You need a zero card. Zeros hit a lot."

The man is banging the machine, and it plays with him a little bit, sending him the FIRST-TWO from time to time, but nothing more than that. In a few minutes, he is down to his last quarter.

The girl says, "Now what?"

He says, "Go get some more money."

She says, "From what?"

"We ain't got no more cash?"

She shakes her head.

He says, "Well. That's—" but he does not finish his thought.

She says, "We can get some from the Visa."

"We got from the Visa a few minutes ago. What about Barbie them money?"

"No," she says. "No."

"But the mortgage."

"Mortgage can wait. I don't wanna touch Barbie them money."

"Mortgage can't wait."

"Why you touched the mortgage money? Stupid. Shit. Why you hadda touch that?"

"I said the mortgage. You said try it."

"That ain't what I said."

"Don't be loud talking me," he says, pressing her mouth closed with his hand. He's the boss here. Broke, but he is the boss. His hand on her mouth. Then he gets up, apology in his eyes, and holds her against his shoulder. She wraps her arms around his substantial waist and says something into his ear that I cannot make out. He nods and looks down at the machine that has taken the money for their mortgage. Then he knits his brows in determination. "We took out like $500 after that. Not counting the Visa. 'Bout $1,200 in cash and $500 on the Visa. But we don't have to worry about that until the 15th. How much we owe Barbie them?"

She says into his neck, "Counting this?"

"Well, we could cash their check. We gotta cash it anyway."

"Yeah. I feel some kind of luck is coming. Go cash it. You got your ID?"

He tells her, "I got it. You sit here on the seat. I'm going to the cash office." And he leaves her and heads over to the casino's cash office, where personal checks can be cashed for a 15 percent fee. Before he gets there, he stops, closes his eyes, and says a silent prayer in the middle of the floor.

It is 3 a.m. on a Saturday morning in September in this South Florida Indian casino, which means I have been watching them for four hours.

They have lost about $1,700 in four hours. All things considered, that's not too bad. I've done worse. With a chin nod and a *whuzzup*, I stop the older man on his way to the cash office. He does the chin nod back.

"Whuzzup, brother," he says. "How you doin'?"

He doesn't really know me, but he's seen me around. You know how it is. You gamble in a place long enough, you get familiar with the faces of the regulars. But I'm blocking his path, and he wants to get to the cash office so he can cash Barbie them check.

I say to him, "I see you and the lovely wife here again tonight. How they treatin' you?"

His shoulders slump. "You know how it is, brother. Them damn machines. I just need to hit them one time. Seems like they fixed against me winning. You know how it is. You pump in and you pump in, but it doesn't pay a thing. If I could just hit one time."

"Yeah, I know about those machines. They make all that damned noise, but they don't pay."

"You got that right. They don't pay. They beat us tonight bad." Grunting. Shaking his head. Hushed tones. "Over $1,700."

"Whooo. That's a lot of money. That's too much money. That's really too much money," I say, looking him straight in the eye.

He reads something in this, and it pisses him off. "You know what?" he begins to say, and he's glaring at me like, Man, get out of my damned way so I can go cash Barbie them check. He looks like he might take a swing at me. But I stand firm until he lowers his eyes and mumbles, "Well. That's. But . . ." without finishing his thought. He knows what I'm saying is true.

"What if I gave you $900 right now to go home?"

"What?"

I open my wallet, which is thick with hundred-dollar bills. I count out nine hundreds. "What if I gave you $900 right now for you and your lovely wife to get out of here tonight? For you to go home and get some sleep. For you to pay your mortgage. You must pay your mortgage. You must pay your bills. My God, man, pay your damn bills. If I gave you this money, would you go home?"

"Brother, if you did that, I would go home," the old man says.

"Go home. You don't owe me anything. Just don't come back here tonight, do you hear me?" I put the money in his hand and close his fingers around it tight. Now he is embracing me, and I am saying to him, this big, sniffling, weeping old man, "Go home. Go home. Take your wife home. Get out of here, and do not let me see you in any of the other casinos tonight either. If I see you in any of the other casinos tonight, don't ever look my way again, you hear me?"

"Yes, I hear you, brother," he says, wiping a tear from his cheek. Suddenly he becomes animated as he recognizes the hat. "Hey. I heard about you, right? You're the bus driver guy from TV. World Championship of Poker. Won all that money in Vegas—"

"And nearly gave it all back. Yeah. That's me."

"Came in second. You had kings full. That Chinese guy had aces full. What a tough break."

"Hmmm." It was a tough break. But I don't like talking about the past. Or Chinese. It gives me an itch attached to a thousand-pound monkey. "Just go home, brother. Sleep tight."

But he won't leave. "How'd you do it, man? How'd you get out? I see you in here all the time, I never see you play."

"I found another addiction, an addiction called love. An addiction called charity. It's not as strong as gambling, but it will do in a pinch. I found my way out. You'd better find yours. Start tonight. Get some sleep tonight. Don't blow my charity."

"I'm out of here. Good meeting you, brother. Thanks."

The old man shoves Barbie them check in his pocket and goes back over to the machines, where his young wife is waiting. He shows her the $900, then points back to me and waves. I wave back at him. And then at the wife, who cannot meet my gaze.

The wife slings her purse over her shoulder and they exit the casino, the wife putting a little extra in the swing of those hips for me.

Ping.

64.

The wife is no stranger to me.

There will be other nights for her and me upstairs in my room before she finds her way out.

I have heard her song and witnessed her dance. I have tasted my own breath on her lips.

You've got to get up and walk a lucky circle around the table, she tells me. Give your cards time to breath. Change your luck. Change your machine. Play the end machine. Kiss the rabbit's foot. No guts, no glory. You've got to be in it to win it. Give me some more money, P. I feel some kind of luck coming.

No, no, I say. That's not luck you're feeling. That's insanity. Collect two consecutive paychecks. Play with your children. Paint the house. Take piano lessons. Put premium unleaded in your car. Make love to your damn husband. Make love to me (and mean it). Go live life. This is not life. This is death. But she won't listen.

I am no longer in love with her, but her body I will keep. She is pretty, you see, and down here in Florida, unlike in Vegas, my supply of hundred-dollar bills is endless.

The pretty girl is a worse degenerate than the old man.

Go home, pretty girl. Go home and never come back. There is nothing in here for you—nothing at all.

Not even charity.

I tell her what I told Missy. I tell her what I told C.L. I tell her what I tell them all. Never come back.

But of course she comes back.

An hour and a half later. I've been expecting her, though when she walks into the lobby area near the elevators to the hotel rooms, looking flustered and carrying a gripsack, I pretend to be preoccupied, playing a quiet game of solitaire. I don't even look up.

"We had a fight," I hear her say.

I didn't ask, and I don't respond. I flip my solitaire cards on the table. I'm worried about the gripsack she's carrying.

"He thinks I got mad, took the car, and went to my sister's house."

I look up. "Barbie them house?"

"You know my sister them?"

No, but I just couldn't resist. I flip another card.

She indicates the gripsack. "I figured I could stay with you tonight."

"Hell no."

"But—"

"I got company."

"Bitch," she calls me, though I am a man. She throws down the gripsack and spews again. "Who the fuck you think you fucking with, bitch?"

Her neck is be-bopping.

She came here thinking she would do me tonight and get a few hundred dollars for it and then do the machines and then go back to her husband after a night well spent. Now she's got her hands on her hips and her torso is angled forward and her mouth is twisted into an ugly shape and her neck is be-bopping, rhythmically, rocking her pretty face back and forth.

"Ugly cowboy hat–wearing punk-ass bitch."

She slaps the cowboy hat off my head onto the table, mucking my solitaire game as security arrives to secure her wrists and elbows.

In the end, rather than see her arrested, which would only result in potentially dangerous husbandly involvement, I resolve things with shrugs and more money. I explain it to security as a lover's quarrel and rent her a room—not in this place, but at the motel down the street— and give her $200 for kiss, kiss make up. (Security gets one each.) The pretty girl is still huffing when I give her the money, but she does accept it and the motel room, too. She storms out of the casino without displaying any of the gratitude she used to when we first met. She's storming out, loudly complaining, "What's $200 to me? After all that I give you, you ugly cowboy hat–wearing mutha—"

Two hundred?

It is never enough with gamblers. Two hundred is two hundred. Plus the nine I gave her old man? That's $1,100. Gamblers have no perspective. The average American works two weeks and doesn't take home $1,100 after taxes.

It's not like she can even spend it in the casino. Her ruckus has gotten her banned from the premises for a month. So she'll get her night's rest in the motel (if she goes there) and when she wakes up she'll have to go to one of the other casinos to blow the money. If she doesn't go home to her old man first and kiss and make up.

If I were still a betting man, I'd lay it on her blowing it at the other casino *before* going home. If I were still a betting man, I'd lay it on her making a deal with the motel manager: If I decide not to sleep here to-night, can I get in cash what he paid for the room? Can I get back half of it at least? Batting those pretty eyes at him.

Or her.

65.

I ride the elevator up to my suite of rooms and find the fat girl waiting in that museum-piece couch outside my door.

The professor is there, too.

I deal with him first.

Ever since he backslid and started playing again, he has been on a nonstop losing streak. He has lost all of his money and now his home. He is teaching part-time at six colleges to make ends meet. But he holds a special place in my heart. I take him aside, away from the fat girl so that she cannot see, and I hand him the checks and the cash. He frowns when he sees what I have given him: checks made out to his bill collectors, as I had promised, and only $300 in cash.

He whispers, "Am I good for another couple hundred at least? I mean, I gotta have at least $500 to make it through."

I must be firm, but I try to soften the blow with humor. I say to him, "Money for gambling I got, huh?"

He smiles weakly. He knows this joke. It's his joke. He's the one who told it to me in the first place. I must be firm with him, but I find another $200 for him in my wallet. He takes it and gets on the elevator. I watch as the elevator doors close and he descends to pay his little bills and gamble.

Then my fat girl, grinning lasciviously, gets up and pats her dress down smooth over the ample curves of her hips. Her greeting is a hug and a kiss on the mouth. She tastes good. She smells good. She always smells good, like freshly cut peach halves.

Now she is climbing my body, trying to wrap her legs behind my back. She wants me to lift her. She is not so fat that I cannot lift her, but I am tired tonight and somewhat bummed after seeing the professor. Seeing him always depresses me, reminds me that no matter how much money I have, it can all be gone in an instant. Seeing him brings back both the itch and the sense of doom, reminds me that underneath it all, I am still a gambler. I fall back against the door, with the fat girl's wet mouth still on mine, and fit the plastic key card into the lock without seeing. When we stumble backwards into the room, she is still grinding against me, but I do not lift her and I hardly kiss back. She soon gets the message and pulls away. Pats down her dress again. Then she gets an idea and snatches the cowboy hat off my head and places it on her own, where it sits high on her throwback Afro.

I laugh and say, "You look good, cowgirl."

I turn to the night table, where I dump my wallet, keys, and the small change from my pocket. When I turn back to the fat girl, she is wearing only the hat.

And lacy black garters.

I am too tired tonight, but now we are both laughing and soon we are rolling on the bed. She always gets to me.

I like the fat girl because she is young, bug-eyed cute, and fun. She can wear you out. Plus, she is not anyone's wife or girlfriend that I know of. She works as a receptionist at the water department, takes nursing classes at the community college, and sings alto in the choir of the Greater Mount Olive Missionary Baptist Church where I go sometimes. She still lives at home with her mother and has a baby (age 12), but no baby daddy. Her game is seven-card stud. They are having a tournament tonight, and I figure that's why she text-messaged me earlier: *where U at??? i'm coming up.*

Translation: *I need money for the entry fee.*

She's on top. She's asking for the fee. Winding her belly on my belly. She still has the cowboy hat on. I put my mouth to her ear: "You're going to have to earn your money tonight, cowgirl. *Ping. Ping.*"

We kiss and proceed to a quickie. A real slow quickie.

Then I give her the money for the entry fee and send her away so I can get some sleep. She takes my cowboy hat for extra luck. She already keeps in her right shoe for luck one of my very, very close Super Bowl losers. But the cowboy hat—everybody wants my cowboy hat.

She comes back to my room about 7:00 in the morning to return the hat and report that she came in second in the tournament. She does not offer me any of the prize money, which probably ended up in the machines anyway. The machines are her second addiction after seven-card stud. I am her third, she has told me, and I like her, so I believe her. She yawns, "Too late to drive home. Too sleepy."

I say, "Hmmm?"

She rests the hat on the bed and looks at me expectantly, like she thinks I think she owes me something. Well, she does owe me money, a lot of money, but we both know she will never pay that back. What she thinks is that I want another roll in the sack. But I am tired and sore. The place where I was shot is hurting again. I am out of Viagra. I put my hand over my mouth. Yawn like I am really sleepy. I want her to go home and rest so she can make good on our deal from last night—

She slips off her shoes and begins to undress.

—or she can just sleep here, I guess.

She goes into the bathroom, and a few minutes later I hear the shower. I hear her singing: "Lead Me to the Rock That Is Higher Than

I." Her voice is rich and mellifluous. She needs no accompaniment. Her voice is enough. It's like listening to the radio. It's beautiful. It's so beautiful I will take her again if she comes back to bed singing. I find myself singing along, though my voice sucks. I sound like a bus driver. I don't want her to hear that. I shut my mouth as soon as the shower turns off, though she continues.

My alto comes back to bed, her skin redolent and glistening with cocoa butter. She wraps an arm around me, gives me a peck on the cheek, and in no time her lips are puttering like a motor against my neck as she begins to snore. For a while, I am humming "Lead Me to the Rock," then I am out, too.

The alarm that wakes us up says it's noon. We dress quickly and hurry downstairs. While valet is retrieving my car, she bums another $20 and runs inside to hit the machine "one last time real quick," she promises.

Five minutes. Ten. Twenty.

When she gets back, I am in the car and frowning. Not because she has lost the $20, which I know without asking, but because she is making me seriously late.

When we get to the Orange Bowl, the first quarter is over. Our side's band is playing the fight song. The score is already 21-0. The fans are going nuts. I ask the guy we sit down next to, "How'd we score?"

He says, "You know it. The wonder kid."

"The two-way player."

"It was beautiful," the guy says, taking out his cigar to explain. "He ran one back. He threw for one. And this last one—busted play, they're in on him, he has nowhere to go, he puts his head down, and he takes off—89 yards! The kid is beautiful, and I got good money riding on the game. Whoo-wee!"

I turn to my fat girl. "See? I told you."

She squeezes my arm. "You ought to be proud."

Yeah. I ought to be. I look across the field to the other side of the stadium, but I do not see his brothers or his mother there. Then a chance glance down and I recognize the back of her head, mostly because of some dangly-dangly earrings she's wearing. Some dangly-dangly earrings I had bought her years ago. I remember the $3,200 jackpot that paid for them.

The crowd cheers and surges to its feet, and my ex-wife and her dangly-dangly earrings disappear into the crush of orange- and green-clad bodies again. I turn back to the game, and our son, our allergy boy—whose allergies are long gone—is running down the field, carrying the ball and two or three defenders, toward the goal line. They stop him this time. A gang tackle. Followed by a late hit. But he gets up strong, brushes it off, and swaggers back to his side of scrimmage. Every player in the huddle's got their hands on him, their champion, the all-star freshman. The way he stands, the way he's built—he reminds me of his grandfather, my father, who was built like a truck. He's built like a smaller truck. A truck without a beer belly. He's wearing the number 13, Marino's number. My dad would have been proud.

This happened not because of me, but despite me, my ex-wife likes to throw in my face. All of the good things. All of the things I should be thankful for. Like my daughter the doctor. Like the older boys—both of whom married nice girls. Both of whom have good jobs. Despite me. But I gambled and I won, can't she see? I am high risk, but I won. I paid for their fancy weddings, their lavish honeymoons, set them up in their big houses. Why didn't they turn all that down?

They're no fools. The way this country is set up—this is no place for the poor. Come on. The credit cards, the bills, driving that bus, taxes.

I'm not trying to defend this thing—this thing is crazy. This thing will kill you if you're not lucky. But I am lucky.

My ex-wife is full of shit.

I may not have been the best father in the world, but my boys know I love them.

I see them now, down there, cheering their brother on.

They are good boys.

Ah, who am I kidding? Maybe she's right. What they've become, what they are as men, I have to admit they've got her and their . . . stepfather to thank for that. He's one of those safe guys. A hard worker. Owns his own business. Born again. The boys work for him. He's in air-conditioning repair, or some crap like that. I'm sure my old in-laws like him just fine. There he is, sitting next to my ex-wife's earrings in his suit. He always wears a suit like he's some big shot. I've got enough cash to buy and sell him a hundred and ten times. He's cheering.

The crowd roars. I am snapped out of my thoughts by the image of my little allergy boy built like my father the truck spiking the ball in the end zone.

Another touchdown!

He raises his hands and begins to dance in celebration. The referee blows the whistle and throws the flag. No showboating, young man. A ten-yard penalty after the kickoff. The crowd boos the referee.

"Screw you, ref!" I shout. "Where were you on that late hit?"

My son's a two-way player, but the coach is going to give him a rest on this kickoff. He shrugs and begins his trot off the field. They're cheering him again. He's got his arms raised. Pumping the air with his fists. I wave my cowboy hat at him. My son stops and scans the crowd. He sees me! He's waving back. My fat girl puts her hand on my back. "That's him," I hear her say.

"That's him," I tell my fat girl. I'm standing on my seat. I'm waving. My son is waving back. I'm brushing back the tears. It is beautiful. It is the happy note. It's like a machine going jackpot. It's like a royal flush in hearts. "That's my boy."

If I were still a betting man, I'd bet on him to score again. I'd bet on his team to win. I'd bet on his team to win every game. I would bet and I would win.

66.

When we get to GA, my fat girl takes her usual seat in the back near the exit and prepares to nod off during the proceedings as she always does. She is not much interested in being rescued from her dangerous vice, which she does not consider a dangerous vice. She is only there because of me. O.C. is in the middle of upbraiding the new guy, D, who is insisting again that he is not addicted to gambling but in desperate need of money—gambling is merely a means to come by it.

D, beefy and college-aged with sandy blond hair pulled back in a ponytail, was caught skimming from the cash registers at the FoodGarden grocers where he was a manager, and they made him come here after his six-month incarceration at the county jail. He is gesturing wildly.

"But I paid back the money."

O.C. says, "You'll just do it again."

"And this will help? Give me a break. Where do you think I got the money to pay them back with? I won it gambling, that's where."

"You can go back to jail."

"I gambled in jail."

"You got the monkey on your back."

"It's no damn monkey, man. What I did was wrong. Stealing is wrong, but I'm not a gambler. I stole because I needed the money."

"Which you then blew at the casino," says O.C. "The gambling will make you do worse than steal. In order to get a grip on your life, you've got to get a grip on the gambling first."

D makes a dismissive gesture with his hand when O.C. tries to put an arm over his shoulder. The others are nodding their heads and saying, "It's the gambling. Yes. Gotta get a grip on the gambling." D shakes his head at them defiantly.

"Take P, for example," says O.C. "P might have something to tell you about what the gambling made him do."

I frown. I don't much like D, who is a windbag.

D frowns. He doesn't much like me either. He tells O.C., "Fuck P."

O.C. says to me, "P, you want to say something helpful to our friend D?"

"Yes. Tell D to go fuck himself."

D says, "Fuck you, P."

"Fuck you, D. Ignore O.C. You should keep gambling until you get lucky like me. I wish you luck, you thieving little weasel."

"Fuck you and the horse you rode in on, P!"

"I rode in on a million-dollar horse in case you didn't notice."

"But you're here just like the rest of us with your cowboy hat."

"You got that right."

"With all your money."

"Amen."

"You're pathetic. You're really pathetic. If I had your kind of money, if any of us had your kind of money, we wouldn't be in here. But look at you. I know about you. I know what you did to your son. I know what you did to your mother."

Low blow. Dead mothers are off limits. Dead sons, too. I say to him,

"But do you know what I did to *your* mother?" I'm looking him dead in his beady, ash-gray eyes. "If she's a gambler and she gambles around here, I probably rode her harder than any horse. In fact, let me take a good look at you. Hey, I think you're my son."

"Fuck you, P." He's coming at me with his fists balled. O.C. is restraining him.

I'm laughing at him.

"Fuck you, P."

"Too late, I'm already fucked. Mmmm. One thing about yo' mama, she sho' 'nuff was good," I say, licking my lips.

"Fuck you, you piece of shit." Now he's breaking out of O.C.'s grip. He's charging right at me. Knocking over chairs. Fists balled. He's a big windbag. He's a pussy.

But so am I.

And I got fists, too.

We're locked onto each other. We're bouncing each other off the walls. The others are shouting. "Break it up! Break it up!" Their arms reach out to grab us.

I hear my fat girl scream, "Hit him, P! Hit him!"

They're pulling us apart. I'm laughing. Huffing. Trying to catch my breath, but laughing, too.

They've got us separated, me and D, got us sitting in chairs facing each other. Everybody surrounding us has their hands on our shoulders to keep us from going at it again. I'm still trying to catch my breath, trying to stop laughing, because I want to say something to D, who's got a real good left. I can feel the whole side of my face swelling from where he hit me. But I got him good, too—there's blood on the ground beneath his chair. My daddy taught me to hit like that. Somebody moves out of the way, and I see that D's bleeding from his nose and from somewhere higher on his head. O.C.'s shaking his head in disapproval. He's saying something about calling the police. He's warning us about the possible legal consequences of our actions. He's warning us never to do something like this again or he will have no choice but to act. He hands D a damp rag and tells him to put it over his face. Someone else says, You need some ice in it, and runs to the fridge to get some ice.

I have caught my breath. I have stopped laughing. I announce: "I want to say something helpful to our friend D."

"No," O.C. says, putting up his hands. "You will say nothing."

I'm trying hard not to start laughing again, but I don't hate D as much now that he's shown me he's got a good left for a pussy, so I restrain my urge to crack a smile or snicker. Instead I plead, "But O.C., that's the whole point of coming here—to share with others of like mind."

"You can share with others of like mind next meeting," warns O.C., "but not tonight. I'm the only one who's going to talk anymore tonight."

"My name is P. I am a gambler."

"Shut up, P! Don't let me have to pick up the phone."

"My name is P. It has been 563 days since I have gambled."

"I'm picking up the phone."

"It has been 563 days. It has been hard—"

O.C. puts his chest in my face and shouts at me, "When I tell you to shut up, you'd better shut the fuck up, P!"

I don't want to tangle with O.C., who was a pro football player and is still in really good shape. But I shout right back at him, "He needs to hear this! My name is P! I am a gambler! I haven't gambled in 563 days! It has been hard! It has been very hard! Despite the fact that I am rich! Despite the fact that I no longer believe in luck! I used to think it was about luck! I used to think it was about wanting to make money! But it's not! It's deeper than that. I want to gamble because I am a gambler."

O.C. sees that I'm not screwing around and steps back. He sees that I'm not playing some kind of prank on D. "Go on, P. Go on," O.C. says, as though he even had a chance in hell of stopping me. No one can stop me tonight. I have to say what I have to say to our friend D.

"I am a gambler, so I gamble. There may have been other reasons to do it back in the beginning when I got started—belief in my own skill or talent, belief in luck, a need for money or excitement or fun—but now I do it because I need it like I need air. I am rescued from it. I don't do it anymore. It has been 563 days. But being rescued from it is the hard part. Being rescued from it is like living death. If you believe in luck, you feel empty when you stop believing. Now you know there is no luck. Now you know that if you play you're probably going to lose because that's just the way it is. That's what gambling is designed to do—make you lose. You know this now. Therefore, you do not play. You no longer believe. But there is that place inside where the belief used to be . . . When you were low, you would go gamble and you would be lifted. When you were depressed, you would go gamble and you would feel good, win or lose, because you were pumped full of the belief, the possibility, that you *might* win. It was exciting. It was your drug. And you felt its effects whether you won or lost. Gambling teaches you to feel good even when you lose. Even if you have a bad day gambling, you are still pumped. A losing day is still better than a day not gambling. The only problem with losing, for a gambler, is that if you lose enough then you can no longer gamble. That's the big problem with losing. It's not about losing money. It's about not being able to gamble until you find some more money to gamble with. It's about waiting for that next paycheck, two long weeks from now. It's about borrowing from friends and family, not to pay bills, but to gamble. It's about stealing—taking money from the registers at FoodGarden, for instance—stealing not to get rich, but so that you can get back to that casino to your drug. Winning is not your drug. Gambling is your drug. Gambling is what lifts you."

"Amen," somebody says. And the others join in. D is holding the rag filled with ice under his nose. The anger has gone out of his eyes.

O.C. tells me, "Go on."

I go on.

"So now you are rescued. But gambling is your drug. Gambling is what lifts you. But now you no longer believe. Now you know better. But you still get low. Now what lifts you when you are low? Nothing. There is no replacement drug for gambling. Sex. Family. Money. Charity. Love. Nothing. The call never goes away. It keeps calling to you. Its voice is sweet. Play, it says, play just a little. You do not believe in it anymore, so you do not play, but you remember how good it felt to be lifted. Win or lose. Nothing can replace that. Nothing can replace what you used to believe. Therefore, you end up believing in nothing."

"Nothing. Nothing."

"Amen. Amen."

"Tell it," says my fat girl.

"That's what pisses you off the most. You let it get out of hand. You let it control you. Now you're not allowed to do it at all. Not even in moderation. All of these little old ladies and tourists and regular people going into casinos every day, betting their little pennies and nickels for fun, and having fun! They bet a few dollars—they lose and leave. Laughing. Oh, what great fun they had. Why couldn't you have been like one of them? Why did you have to go and let it control you? What made you so different from everybody else? What?"

"What, Lord? What?"

"Amen. Amen."

"Preach it," says my fat girl, clapping. "Tell it."

"So now you're cured. All being cured means is you don't scratch anymore. But nothing ever gets rid of the itch. You itch all the time, but you do not scratch because you are cured. What kind of hell is that? My God, I'm itching. I'm itching every day."

"Lord."

"Help us, Lord."

"Amen."

"I went to my boy's game today. He was wearing the number 13. Now I am seeing the number 13 everywhere I go. I see it on license plates. I see it on street signs. I do not believe that if I play this number in the Cash-3 that it will hit tonight. I do not believe that if I play it on the machines that it will play. I do not believe that if I play it in the lottery this weekend that it will hit. But I am seeing it. It is calling to me. Its voice is sweet. If it plays in the Cash-3 tonight, it has nothing to do with the fact that it was on my son's helmet. I know this. I know this. I know this. The payoff is 500-to-1. I don't need the money. I've got millions, but wouldn't that be awesome? It would lift me, D. I would be so high."

O.C. is doing his best to stop it, but they're all saying, "That would be awesome. That would surely be awesome."

The fat girl is saying it. "That would be awesome. Amen."

D has that rag full of ice to his face, and he is saying it, and he's not thinking about how he'd be able to pay off all his little debts, he's not thinking about how he wouldn't have to work at a dead-end job anymore—he's not thinking like that, he's not thinking like a chump, he's thinking like a gambler—he's thinking wouldn't it be awesome to put everything he owns in the world on a 500-to-1 Cash-3 and feel that high when those numbers come in. Or not.

I know where he's coming from. I'm thinking it, too, even though I no longer believe.

O.C. is trying his best, but the place is out of control. O.C. is not happy about it. I address the frowning O.C. and I tell him, "Sorry, man, sorry to mess up your meeting like this, but it *would* be awesome. It really would be. And I know that you know it. I see through your face. I see through your stone face. I see your tells. You itch, O.C. You want to scratch. What's wrong with a little scratch? You know it would be awesome. You know it would be. It would make you so happy. It would make me so happy. It would make us all so happy. Sing it with me like you know how to sing, *ping-ping, ping-ping.* This is our happy note, O.C. What's so wrong with being happy?"

PART V
Murder

This Is My Corinthians

He lived a gambler's dream. He gambled millions of dollars at a time. What a high that was. What a high.

—C.L.

Though I speak with the tongues of men and angels, and have not charity, I am become as a sounding brass, or a tinkling cymbal. And though I have the gift of prophecy, and understand all mysteries, and all knowledge; and though I have all faith, so that I could remove mountains, and have not charity, I am nothing. And though I bestow all my goods to feed the poor, and though I give my body to be burned, and have not charity, it profiteth me nothing. Charity suffereth long, and is kind; charity envieth not; charity vaunteth not itself, is not puffed up, doth not behave itself unseemly, seeketh not her own, is not easily provoked, thinketh no evil; rejoiceth not in iniquity, but rejoiceth in the truth; beareth all things, believeth all things, hopeth all things, endureth all things. Charity never faileth.

—1 Corinthians 13

I am impatient. I am unkind. I envy those who win. I want them to lose. Always. I am puffed up. I behave unseemly. I am selfish. I am easily provoked. I have evil thoughts on my mind. Always. I rejoice *in the wickedness of my ways. I am in denial. Something is wrong with me, but I can't take knowing that something is wrong with me. I believe in nothing anymore. I have no dreams, no ambitions, except to keep playing. I hate myself. Hate? I loathe myself. I am weak. I am a failure. This is my Corinthians.*

—P

The only addiction stronger than gambling is charity.

—O.C.

Bullshit.

—P

Go to hell, P.

—O.C.

I am in hell.

—P

67.

His phone rings in the middle of the night, but he does not reach over and pick it up from the nightstand, answering it groggily from sleep. When his phone rings in the middle of the night, it is a cell phone, and he retrieves it from his pocket and answers it quite soberly, for he is a gambler and wide awake at a casino playing the machines. *Ping-ping.*

"Hello," he says.

"Professor."

"P! Where are you?"

"You know I can't tell you that."

"Are you all right? I saw it in the news."

"I'm all right for now."

"P . . ."

"Look, here's the deal, what about lesbians?"

"Lesbians?" The professor is completely baffled. "P, are you okay? Do you want me to help you with this?"

"Lesbians have roundness," P says.

The professor stops pressing PLAY. Now he understands. He says into the phone shouldered to his ear, "Yes. Lesbians, as all other women, have roundness. Men are still attracted to their roundness. It is the lesbian who is not attracted to the man. Now, this has interesting ramifications."

"Ramifications," P says. His voice is trembling.

"Well," the professor says, selecting his words with care, "this means that, if she chooses, she can still display her roundness to profitable effect as far as males are concerned. She can, if she chooses, profit from her roundness in the same manner as all females. In most cases, she simply chooses not to because, for various reasons, she is unaffected by or perhaps repulsed by the male form. In fact, she herself is attracted to roundness."

"It's a shitty theory."

"P . . . my God, P."

"I think what it is, is that we are equally attracted to each other. We are attracted to their roundness, but maybe they're just as attracted to our . . . muscles or whatever. Girls get turned on, too, right?" P sobs.

"P."

Then silence.

"P?"

"What about hookers?" he asks.

The professor sighs. What's the use? "The hooker, okay," he says. "Good one. The hooker. In fact, the hooker is a direct and very obvious application of the theory. The hooker has roundness that she profits from. Men pay her for the pleasure of relieving themselves in her roundness, and like the lesbian, the hooker may very well be otherwise repulsed by the male. On the other hand, the hooker may be fooling us all. She may very well be using her roundness for financial profit and gaining much sexual gratification from it at the same time. In other words, she can have the best of both worlds anytime she chooses."

"Is the casino a hooker or a lesbian?"

"P, I can help you. I know people."

"I don't think I like your theory, professor, but I see your point. She is unaffected by me. She is round and curvy and I am attracted to her, but she does not like me. She gives me a good time for my money, all of my money, but really she is repulsed by me."

"There is still hope. The boy is not dead."

"Aha! The casino is a bisexual hooker. Her roundness attracts women, too. I've seen it. I've seen it!" he suddenly shouts.

"P! P!" the professor cries, as his phone goes silent because P has hung up.

The professor, who is not a religious man, utters an earnest prayer for P as he replaces his phone in his pocket. Then he changes his numbers on the screen and begins to press PLAY again. *Ping-ping.*

68.

Not a day went by that Missy did not think of her black man.

With each glance back, he grew wiser, nobler, more handsome. The con had become in her mind less a con and more a grand gesture. He had saved her. He had turned her life around. It was only in retrospect that she could admit that she had come perilously close to ruining her career (so many missed days, so many missed deadlines) and losing her family (the fifteen-year-old was sexually active, the thirteen-year-old had been experimenting with marijuana and satanic body art). And her finances—how could a professional woman who made so much have so little? She was maxed out on everything, she owed everybody, and when she got brave and tallied all the receipts, earnestly, she discovered that she had blown close to $200,000 in her year and a half of sooth-ing, relaxing, stress-relieving gambling at the sweet, innocent, harm-less low-stakes Indian casinos of South Florida. She had been blowing money at a rate of a little over $10,000 a month. She couldn't believe it. No wonder the $10,000 jackpot that she had gotten so exited about didn't last more than 30 days. No wonder she didn't have a pot to piss in despite her six-figure salary. So that was addiction and she hadn't even noticed.

Now she was addicted to the memory of the man who had saved her. (She was not in love with him, per se. She was seeing her personal trainer again, seeing him in more than one sense of the word this time, Ricardo, with his Latin complexion and his addiction to setting goals both in bed and out. She had lost 20 pounds so far.) The gambler who had saved her, she cherished the feel of him that she carried in her heart. It colored everything.

Of late, she had begun researching gambling and addiction.

She had put out a call for manuscripts and had persuaded her bosses to devote the house's resources to no fewer than three projects on gam-bling next season: a coffee table book on casinos, a how-to guide for beginning poker players, and a fictional book whose protagonist was a gambler, though she had not found an author or an outline for that one yet.

She had researched the man himself and come up with very little. Many of the gamblers she interviewed knew of P, the bus driver, the man in the black cowboy hat, and they all had stories to tell—oh, what stories they told—but as far as printed material was concerned, she had unearthed a mere half dozen photographs from his days as a professional in Las Vegas and an interview he had done for the online magazine TheGambleToday.com during the finals of the World Championship of Poker a few years back.

Three months later, on the morning of December 5, Missy's final red-lining of a manuscript was interrupted by a buzz from her secretary. It was a bicycle messenger with a letter. It was from *him*:

Missy, you said you wanted to know who I was and my friends tell me you have been asking around about me. Here is your opportunity. Take this key to ___'s Storage. There you shall find all you need to know about P. You are beautiful. I enjoyed our time together. I am happy that I don't see you around the casinos anymore. That is the best sign of all. Be strong. Be strong every day and night for the rest of your life. Never let your guard down. It will call you again. I will call you nevermore. P.

69.

When she got to ___'s Storage, she went to unit 323, which was one of the closet-sized ones. She found inside four lawn bags filled with ATM receipts; an envelope with a handful of old lottery tickets in it, Play-4 tickets, all of them with the same number, 7-9-7-9; a handwritten note;

a handwritten manuscript in a shoebox; a note card of lucky numbers; and a black cowboy hat. *His* cowboy hat. She read the handwritten note:

By the time you read this I will be dead. There are two things you need to know about me from when we met in September. First, I was down to my last couple million. That may sound like a lot to you. It is not to a man who has had a hundred times that much pass through his hands. Second, you are a most attractive woman, though I approached you not because of your beauty, but because I found out through friends that you were an editor and thought that one day I might need someone like you to handle my story, which you shall find in the box. This is not to say that our encounter was a plot, or a ruse, for there is not a day that has passed that I have not thought of you. It is simply that I wanted this business to be handled by someone who had experienced me firsthand. Outsiders do not understand us. They would hold up my manuscript for its prurience, or they would use it to sermonize, or they would make of it a tragedy. Addiction is not a tragedy; it is a love story with abuse in it. We love, and it abuses us. I was rescued from it for a while, for 564 days, but in the end I reverted to type and started making trips back to Vegas. I wanted to get back some of what I had lost. Mostly, I wanted to hear the ping-ping. I wanted to breathe. You know how it is. The final three months of my life was an unending string of abuse by it upon my person. How do you say unbelievable bad luck? You know what I'm talking about. You have been there.

As to my death, I shall be brief. After we met, the itch hit me hard. I went to my son's game. I went to my final GA meeting. I went back to Vegas. I stayed too long. Less than a week ago, when I blew the final penny of my money, I came back to Miami and sought out my son, who is in his first year at the University of Miami. In a saner frame of mind, I had given him a sum, half a million, to hold for just in case. I demanded it. He refused, seeing the state that I was in. We argued. I had a gun. He will live, I have learned, but his career as an athlete is over. Seeing him like that, I sank into my deepest depression. I still had the gun. The rest you can figure out.

Please do not include the tragedy in the book. I want it to end on a happy note, though I do not know how that will be possible. Perhaps you can end it on that night in Vegas when I slept with my wife. That was a happy note. I recall that I was happy. See to it that the proceeds, if there are any, go to my ex-wife, my children, and the friends listed herein. I beg of you not to reveal my name and embarrass anyone that I have met in this wretched happy life I have lived.

Oh, Missy, I am sad, so sad. I have never felt this low in my life. And so tired. I am tired of being tired. I'm tired of feeling like I'm running up a steep hill with lead in my shoes and a big old heifer on my back. I am looking forward to not being tired. I just feel as though I've lived my entire life running and hiding like some criminal. I'm tired of lying. I'm tired of running. I'm tired of it all. I'm tired of feeling what I'm feeling right now. I want to gamble. In prison there are no casinos. I can't live like that, Missy. I refuse to live like that. P.

70.

(P's Lucky Numbers)

123

323

262

232
626
646
464
797
979
585
858
989
898
373
737
621
261
908

Fantasy 5: 12, 13, 23, 26, 29 (backup combos: switch out each number with 1 and then 11). Lotto: 23, 26, 32, 37, 41, 46 (backup combos: switch out the 41 with 1, 13, 17, 19, and 21).

71.

(She found it scrawled on the back of the card, barely legible.)

the fifth definition of insanity: we pass it on to our children and they accept it without question—this is how we hurt them, this is how we destroy the future P

(She found an ATM receipt with some kind of poem scribbled on it in pencil,)

A Poem for P

There is only one man I love
And it is you
On the weekends when you don't drive me
I am blue . . .

(and she flipped through the manuscript pages to get a feel for his voice.)

. . . now, as far as religion is concerned, I am not the most religious guy in the world. I was raised in a Christian home, so that's where my head's at for all intents and purposes. The thing is, well, I'm no philosopher, I'm a school bus driver, but from my way of looking at it, a long, long time ago you got these desert people with their turbans and their camels and some of them are shepherds with no sense of how the world really works, no concept of science—and we get our information about God and the creation of the world from them?

On the other hand, when I'm in a tough spot, I pray. There are no atheists in a casino. I pray, I pray my butt off—and something usually happens and I'm out of the tough spot.

I'm all-in, Lord. The only card that can help me is the nine of clubs, Lord.

And blam! There's the nine of clubs.

Now, what does all that mean? Did God give me the winning card? Is God a gambler? Does God have a monkey on his back, too? Does the monkey preach the gospel? I don't know. But I'll tell you this, I was sitting in seat number three when this Omar Sharif—

looking Middle Eastern dealer hit me with that first royal flush.

I took note of that.

My second royal, this was a few weeks later, I was sitting in seat three again. The guy gave me four face-card hearts, minus the jack. I'm thinking, Can lightning strike twice? What are you saying to me, Lord? A royal flush is the rarest of all hands. The odds are something like 280,000 to 1. Sure enough, the dealer popped me the jack of hearts. Another royal. This time the Indians were giving away $1,199 for each royal. So I tipped the dealer $100 and gave everyone else a 20.

I started to like seat three. I started doing things to get it, like coming to tournaments early. Paying other players a few bucks to swap with me. They started calling me Seat Three. It got to the point where I'd skip a tournament sometimes if I couldn't get my beloved seat three. But I'm a different kind of true believer. My religion is gambling. I got to play, I got to play, I got to play, Amen, so give me a seat. Any seat. I'm in church, y'all.

There is power, power,
Wonder working power,
In the cards,
    (in the cards!)
In my hand,
    (in my hand!)

There is power, power,
Wonder working power,
In the precious cards in my hand.

So then I hit again, in seat seven this time, and of course seat seven in a nine-handed game is three seats away from the dealer. So now I'm thinking, *That's the answer. The Lord is telling me I have to be three seats away from the dealer to get these royals.* So now I can sit in seat three or seven. That opened up more playing opportunities for me. I skipped fewer tournaments.

I went to the other casino down in the swamp to spend a romantic weekend there with my wife. The first night I was there, I told the dealer, "I'm in my lucky seat, bro. Seat three. This is my royal flush seat. Deal me that royal. Thus sayeth the Lord."

He laughed and dealt me a royal flush on the next hand. Everyone was amazed. This time the jackpot was up to $2,500. So I tipped the dealer $250 and gave everyone else $25. Nice.

My biggest royal, however, was not in seat three.

There was this time I was in a tournament and I couldn't manage to get seat three. Back then you had to pay an extra three bucks if you wanted to try for the royal during the tournament. If you didn't pay the three bucks and a royal was dealt to you, you got nothing, just the pot and a baseball cap with the casino's name on it. Since I had been unable to get my beloved seat three, I decided not to pay the three bucks. On the second hand, I'm dealt four face-card diamonds. The jackpot was up to $14,222. I said to the dealer, "Whatever you do, don't break my heart. Don't deal me the 10 of diamonds. I didn't pay the three bucks for the royal." The kid smiled and proceeded to deal me a 10 of diamonds. I sat there crying at the poker table so hard they had to interrupt the tournament to straighten me out. Everybody was sad for me. When the pit boss came around and gave me my prize, the stinking baseball cap, I begged him with the tears still in my eyes to accept the three bucks late. Please. Please. He informed me sadly, "Rules is rules."

Is there a God? Is there a God who would allow a thing like that? What kind of rules are those? Is there someone up there working against us? A real gambler, no matter how lucky he is, has no luck at all. Everything in this world is fixed against him.

One day, I found myself in seat 10. I hate seat 10. You're right next to the dealer. Some of them smell bad. They work all night or all day some of them. This guy, thank God, smelled nice. He was one of my favorite dealers. He was good-natured and he controlled the action at the table with a firm but fair hand, which is all you can ask of a dealer. As he dealt he was making these self-deprecating jokes about how he hadn't dealt a royal in like over a year. The jackpot was up to $6,998. I looked down and saw that I had four face-card diamonds. I said to the friendly dealer, "Just give me the king of diamonds and you're gonna have six hundred bucks in your hand." He dealt me the king of diamonds on the last card. I fell out of my chair. It was crazy. I tipped the guy the six hundred. I gave everyone at the table fifty. It was a good morning for me.

I don't worry about seat three or seat seven anymore. Superstitions are crazy. Imagine if I had fought for seat three that day. Imagine if I had been the other kind of true believer. I don't even want to think about it. Thank God I'm not a zealot.

(She set the manuscript down, and then she wept.)

72.

(He Paid His Tithes)

Missy attended his funeral, which was held on a Saturday in a mid-sized Baptist church in the north end of Miami. It was a closed-casket affair as are most suicides of this sort in which the head is deformed by the entry and exit wounds. Mounted on the coffin was an oversized photograph of him. He was smiling. He was wearing his black cowboy hat. There were many wreaths of flowers layered upon each other in a brightly colored heap of fragrance and petals. The officiating minister gave a surprisingly robust, cheerful eulogy for P, which was well-received by all in attendance—but that of course was the problem. His ex-wife was not there, nor was the son whom P had assaulted. Missy found out from one of P's sisters that the boy had recovered enough to have attended but had decided not to. Also missing was one of the other two sons, the middle boy. Thus, P's nearest kin at the funeral were his sisters, his daughter, and the eldest of his remaining sons, a sleepy-eyed man in his early 20s who bore a striking resemblance to him. A highlight of the ceremony was the tearful solo singing of a hymn, "When My Heart Is Overwhelmed, Lead Me to the Rock That Is Higher Than I," by a chubby, somber woman who later introduced herself to Missy as P's girlfriend. There were several such women who introduced themselves thus, or as his exes. Missy realized, with a smirk, that she could have included herself in this group.

The officiating minister set the crowd to chanting Amen when he said, "There was none more generous than P. He gave with his heart and he never asked for it back. He was what he was and he lived what he lived. His life was a blessing to us all. He showered us with blessings. He paid his tithes." The minister never once mentioned anything remotely close to the word *gambler* in his eulogy. Missy was aware that many in the large crowd at the funeral were gamblers. They sure looked like gamblers. They were a shady bunch. Many of them were tattooed.

The interment was held at a graveyard a few miles away from the church. It took the long chain of cars a full half hour to snake its way into the cemetery. At the graveside, P's daughter, listed in the obituary as Dr. _____, a pediatrician, collapsed and began to wail, "Daddy, Daddy, Daddy, oh Daddy." The tall, handsome man, her husband, helped her back to her feet. Missy noted that the toddler clutching the daughter's hand, P's grandson, was listed in the obituary as P _____ III, and she was suddenly overcome with sadness.

73.

After the ceremony, Missy found that the gamblers, especially those who stood to benefit from the book, were eager to talk to her once she had explained who she was and her purpose for being there.

A dapper, well-dressed gambler introduced himself as Professor _____ and began to speak: "He died virtually penniless and yet he left me five grand to help me out. What a guy. He didn't have to do that, but that's the way he was. I'll tell you one thing, he didn't mean to shoot his boy. This thing makes you crazy. What a tragedy, what a tragedy. See, if it actually paid off the way it should, most of us here would be doing all right. We are good at it, we know all the angles, we play it right, but it is fixed against us. The problem is that these machines down here are not slot machines. These machines down here are video pull-tabs, which means that no matter how much you play them, the chances are pretty good that you are not going to win. You know why? A pull-tab is a scratch-off. Thus, a video pull-tab is a video scratch-off. That means, just like in the scratch-off games you buy in the grocery stores, the winner is already predetermined. So let's say that you live in Miami, but the winning ticket has been printed in Orlando. Well, you can buy as many scratch-off tickets as you want, there is no way for you to win because the winning ticket is not even in your city . . ." The professor went on long after Missy had lost interest and stopped taking notes.

Missy was surprised to bump into the former number-three NFL draft choice O.C. in attendance at P's funeral. "His death is typical," explained O.C. "It should be a warning to everyone who thinks that this thing is innocent. I've seen guys richer than him lose it all. The rich ones are the hardest to convince. They think that there is no way that they can lose all that—they've got millions. It happens and then they do this. The thing with P is, he fooled us. A guy hits rock bottom you can help him. There was no way to help P, but we didn't know that. He had us fooled. That's what made him different from the rest of us all along. What I'm saying is, P *never* hit rock bottom. He got close, but he never hit it. You hit rock bottom, you can be helped. Every time he got close, he would win again, so he couldn't be helped. He had too much luck—the lucky ones are just as hard as the rich ones to convince. The twelve steps are useless to them. P probably wasn't even listening to us. This time his luck ran out. He hit rock bottom for real and see what happened? He learned his lesson, tragically. It's very sad, but typical."

On that dark day Missy interviewed about a dozen of them in all, men and women, black and white (and Chinese), gamblers who had known and loved P in his short, "tragic" life. There was enough here now for her to put in the book, but she couldn't shake the feeling that she was still missing something. The gentle spirit that was P, how could he do a thing like this? It is not typical of him. Perhaps she should try again to interview the family, who had all already turned her down, but it wasn't about family—it was about gambling.

Then the thin, sad, pretty woman approached her. She introduced herself as C.L. and explained that she was in a recovery program and that it had been 100 days since she had last gambled and that she had been advised by her counselor not to attend the funeral because it might lead to a relapse, her being in the company of so many gamblers.

"Degenerates," C.L. called them, "like I used to be, but no way in hell was I gonna miss his funer—"

As the pretty C.L. broke down in tears, Missy could not help but feel a twinge of jealousy. This was the same C.L. that P had written about with such passion. This was the same C.L. whom P had loved. This was his partner. C.L. herself was there with a partner, a handsome light-haired butch in a dark suit whom she introduced as Maggie.

When C.L. got herself back together, she said, "When you write about P, don't get all sappy. If you get all sappy, then you don't understand P at all. P had fun. It wasn't a nightmare for him. No way. He lived a gambler's dream. He gambled millions of dollars at a time. What a high that was. What a high. What fun he had. Sweet Jesus."

"Fun?" Missy said. "He shot his own son. He shot himself."

C.L. snapped back angrily, "He had fun! That's what it's all about! And when it was over, nothing else made sense. There was no point in doing anything else. I don't know about you, but it makes perfect sense to me. And then his son wouldn't give him the money. It's the son's fault he's dead! I mean, he's your father, you've got to give him the money. Let him take his chances with it, let him try to turn it into something. It's only money. P is lucky. P could have done it. P would have turned it around if the kid had just given him that money."

C.L. looked as if she were about to say more, and Missy wanted to hear more, but the other woman, Maggie, put a hand on C.L.'s shoulder and C.L. said an abrupt goodbye and was led away by her partner, leaving Missy alone with her thoughts.

Another gambler, whom she had already interviewed, came to her and invited her to a friendly game of poker that they were having at the professor's place in memory of P, but Missy declined. She had work to do. She had thoughts to think.

74.

(The Monkey's Revenge)

At best it will be a tough sell. There are so many of these books out there now, and not all of them are doing well," her boss tells her. "America, I think, is moving on to other interests. We may be too late on this."

Missy laughs. "Actually, it would be good news for us all if America moves on." On her desk is a mock-up of the book jacket: two hands holding a royal flush in spades. The hands holding the cards are white. P's hands are black, of course. She will tell the artist to darken the hands. There is still time for a cover change. The book will be released in two months. But no. What is she thinking? White hands are an eas-ier sell. "But I feel strongly about this one," she says to her boss. "It gets to the heart of what this thing is. The insanity of it."

Her boss nods as though he understands, but of course he does not.

"Damnit," she suddenly curses. "Damnit, this is hard." Her finger is moving again. She hides it under her desk, hoping her boss did not see.

She keeps it under her desk until he leaves her office. Then when she is alone again, she retrieves it from hiding and says to herself, "It's no use."

She studies her desk calendar, her thoughts drifting back to the old days.

She still awakens at night from dreams about numbers.

The patterns are so clear. So elegant.

She finds herself making love to Ricardo and her head is full of numbers. She comes hard. She comes thinking of numbers. There is money in her bank account. Her debt is at a manageable level now. Yes, her children love her now. Yes, her children *know* her now. These are all good things, and she will not go. She will not go, but P was right—the casino still calls to her.

This is the price that she must pay—must she pay it forever? Nothing is truly interesting or engaging anymore. Nothing. Now she sees the world through dark shades, a world that is permanently lacking in brilliance. Her sun and her moon are in the casino, but she does not go there anymore.

She will *not* go!

Sometimes when her children are talking to her, she is only half listening to them, her breathing shallow, her heart rate soaring, her eardrums reverberating to the sound of the *ping-ping*, her finger pushing the absent *PLAY* button over and over again.

Her children stop talking abruptly. They're looking at her finger now. She sees the look on their faces. She gets a grip on herself. Her finger stops moving.

"Get a grip, get a grip," she says out loud. "It's just no use. No use."

And now her chest is heaving. There are sobs and tears and a physical collapse her children can't possibly understand, but they hug and kiss and say, It's okay, Mommy, it's okay, we're here for you, Mommy. And that should be enough, but really it's not, because tomorrow will be yet another day without gambling.

For Missy sitting at her desk, tomorrow will be 365 days since she last gambled.

"It's just . . . it's just . . ."

Tomorrow will be 365 days since she saw him alive.

"It's . . ." She is resigned to misery.

A whole year has passed, and not a day has gone by in which she has not dreamt about numbers. Numbers that should win—if she would just go. If she would just risk a 20. That's not so much. Now you're just being ridiculous. It's *your* money. It's one lone 20. Go, Missy, go, the monkey says. Go to the casino. It will be so much fun. You really should go, you know. But if you do not go, that's fine, I'll just have to remind you *again* tomorrow. And tomorrow. And tomorrow.

And tomorrow.

At her desk, Missy sobs, "It's insane. It's just insane."

. . . as her finger, of its own accord, begins to push *PLAY*.

75.

On the 365th day, Missy got the break she needed. The son agreed to see her.

It was September, fall again, the start of the new semester, and he was back on campus and back on the team, though he was no longer a starter.

She met him in his dorm. It was pretty much the average young man's college room: bed, desk, and posters of voluptuous, scantily clad *Maxim* women. Next to the deck of cards on the table was an open carton of strawberries he seemed to have been eating before she arrived and a photograph of him and his father taken when he was about 12 or 13.

His old crutches were abandoned in a corner of the room. P's son, a boy with considerable physical presence, had answered the door standing on his own. He was walking again, though with a noticeable favoring of the right leg. He went back to the bed and propped himself up on a pillow. He was a well-mannered boy, who had shaken her hand and offered her something to drink. She had accepted the glass of Gatorade, though she set it down without drinking. He was a handsome boy, about a half shade darker than his father and a half inch taller, and with a body chiseled to the "athletic perfection" described in the article in the sports section: "Indian Casino Regular Shoots Football Star Son." His eyes were the beautiful golden-brown of autumn, his head was clean shaven, and in each ear there was the glint of gold from unmatched earrings. He wore baggy shorts, but from the waist up he was bare. His chest and arms were indeed . . . *chiseled athletic perfection.* Missy willed herself not to stare. She sat down in the chair he offered and focused on his wounds instead. One bullet had shattered the thigh; the other had gone through the shoulder. The healing had been slow and painful, she had heard, but he was strong-willed. Now, except for that limp, he was fine. He had kept in shape, and he could still run quite fast, perhaps not fast enough to play ball at the collegiate level ever again, they had said, but this was a kid who did not know the meaning of the word *fold.* Though he was no longer a starter, not yet, he was a solid second-string and special-teams player. But the shoulder wound—it was familiar and Missy wondered at it.

He shifted his weight on the pillow and stretched out both his long, muscular legs on the bed and recounted the sequence in a tone that was surprisingly childlike:

"I went to see him at his suite in that casino. I knew what he wanted. My mom had told me not to go, but I was his favorite. I always stood up for him. He could do no wrong in my eyes. When I was a kid, he was the one who used to take care of me when I was sick. My most common memory of childhood is me being in the car and him driving me to the emergency room for my asthma and assorted allergies. You don't know what it's like to look up and see your dad's got a gun pointed at you."

He lifted a strawberry from the open carton and popped it in his mouth and chewed.

"I'm telling him, Then go ahead and shoot me then if this is all I mean to you, but I'm not giving you that money. And I'm looking at him, and it's like he's not even my dad anymore. I'm scared because now I don't know who this crazy man is pointing the gun at me. So I make a quick move to run out of the room, and he fired. Twice. I caught the first one right here." He rolled up a leg of his shorts so that she could better see the scar. He traced it with fingers red-tipped from the juice of strawberries. He said, "It rocked me. *Blam*. Then as I was going down, I kinda twisted around and reached my arms out to him. I'm like screaming, Daddy, you just shot me, and *blam*, the next one caught me in the shoulder. Never heard nothing so loud. Never felt nothing hurt so bad. I'm on the ground, I'm shot, and my dad is still shooting at me. I can't believe it. I know he's gonna kill me now for sure. My own father. Because I wouldn't give him that money. So I start telling him how to get it. I'm no punk, but I'm hurting bad. I don't want to die. I want to live. I'm trying to recite the bank account number so he won't shoot me again. But it's all coming out confused because I'm kinda trippin', kinda blackin' out from the pain. I can smell the gunshot. Then he's on the ground with me, he's sobbing, and my head is on his chest, and he's holding me and telling me not to worry, he ain't gonna shoot me no more. Called me his lucky boy. He stayed with me until the hotel security guards got there. They were like kind of his friends, you know? He made some kind of deal with them to get away from the cops and then he threw some clothes in a bag and bailed out of there. Two days later, they found him dead . . ."

His voice trailed off as he lost himself in thought.

"Why didn't you just give him the money?"

"I didn't want him to be what they said he was. I wish I had given it to him. He would still be alive today. Except for this screwed-up thing he did, he was a good father, you know? He was nice. He was funny. He was cool. He would let you slide. He was like that. I have no father now. My daddy's dead."

He looked at her with a helpless expression on his face, and Missy *almost* bought it.

She said to him, "Do you gamble?"

"What?"

"Do you gamble?"

"A little." Ah. The wilting gaze. The glint in his eye. The red fingers reaching for another strawberry. "I play cards with the fellas. The horses," he explained, chewing. "But I win all the time. I'm lucky."

Lucky.

She said to the lucky boy, "How much of the money that he gave you to hold did you lose?" She watched as he put another strawberry to his lips without answering, then pushed it into his mouth. She watched as he shook his head. She closed her notepad and prepared to leave. "You don't have to answer. I understand."

"About $200,000."

"*Two* hundred thousand?" Despite herself, she whistled. "You told him that, and he shot you."

The boy chewed his strawberry. He did not answer.

"You're so young. That's so much money."

"But he's my *father*," the boy said at last. "If he had just given me a few days, I could have won it all back. He shot me."

"Oh my." She understood it now.

"Oh my, my butt. He shot me."

"No. The first time was a mistake because you ran. The second time, he was trying to shoot you in the chest."

"Trying to kill me," he accused.

"He was trying to shoot you like he was shot. He was trying to show you. See?" She cocked a finger like a gun at his wound.

He lowered his head.

"Don't gamble anymore."

"I don't gamble, I told you. I ain't no gambler." With his head lowered and the tremor in his voice.

"How much of the money is left?"

He groaned.

"How much?"

"About . . . $50,000. Forty," he sighed. "That's all that's left."

"That's still a lot of money."

"No it's not," came the sad reply. "I blew it. It was so much, and now it's so little." He was quiet again. His face covered by his hands. He was lost in his gambler's thoughts, Missy knew. His miserable gambler's thoughts. Numbers in his head. His body made small trembling movements. After a long while, he lifted his head and said with finality, "You're gonna put this in that book of yours."

"The book has already been written. That's not why I'm here."

The boy sniffled. "Why *are* you here?"

"Because of P." She got up from her chair and went over to him. "He wanted you to have a chance against this thing. You have no idea how much he loved you. It's not going to be easy, I can't lie to you. But you've got to get help. The first step is to tell someone about it. You need to tell your mother about it—when you are strong enough. And give the money to her. Give the rest of the money to your mother. Let her handle it. She'll know what to do with it . . . Or you'll blow that, too."

The boy nodded. "Yeah. You know how we are."

She smiled. Yes. She knew how they were.

His eyes were misty and there were still tears on his cheeks. Missy put her hand on his face. He looked so much like his father. For a brief moment, she imagined there was a cowboy hat on his head. He seemed to come to a decision about something. He reached over to the table, picked up the deck next to the strawberries, and handed it to her. Missy held P's solitaire deck while his son took out a checkbook and wrote a check to his mother, which he handed to her.

It was a check for $38,271.24. Just like his father, he knew the amount down to the last penny.

"That's all that's left. That's every penny. Give it to her for me. I can't talk to her. I can't do it. Not yet. You know how it is."

"Yes."

She took the check and the solitaire deck and left P's son's room.

But it was such a large check.

There were places that she knew of where people could do things with this check. They could find ways to turn it into cash. By the time the boy figured out what had happened, she would have won all of it back and more. She would share it with him. He would understand. In fact, he would be grateful that she had done it. This is what the monkey told her, this and much, much more, and she drove to the casino and sat in the parking lot in her car, her heart racing. It had been such a long time. She sat in her car and watched the happy ones enter, and the beaten ones exit, with baffled or disgusted expressions on their faces, mumbling promises to themselves that they knew full well they could not keep. It was all so familiar. She could breathe again. The sun shone like a jewel in the sky. The monkey, damn him, was right. She was home again. She was alive.

What's the harm? said the monkey. See? See?

She sat there in her car and breathed. She breathed. She breathed.

Later that day, she dropped the check in the boy's mother's mailbox with a note explaining what it was all about. She closed it with:

> . . . *He has a tough road ahead of him. This thing is hard to get through, much harder to get through alone, but he can depend on me. I will be there for him. I owe that much to his father. This is not a defeat; this is a victory. We have to fight for the rest of our lives to make sure that it is a permanent victory for him.* —Missy

She rang the doorbell and then dashed back to her car, where she waited until the mother opened the door and retrieved the large envelope she found sticking out of her mailbox. As the mother read the note, her hand flew up and covered her mouth. A look of shock stiffened her face. Her cheeks became shiny with tears.

Missy saw all this and said to the monkey, See? See?

And then she sped away.

ACKNOWLEDGMENTS

The author would like to thank Joseph McNair, Leejay Kline, Louise Skellings, Joseph Steinmetz, Gonzalo Barr, Elizabeth Cox, David Beatty, Ariel Gonzalez, Cameron A. Allen, Sherwin D. Allen (Chief), Anna Ashley, my editor Katie Blount at Akashic Books, and the real-life gamblers whose daily struggles are set down herein.

Much props to Johnny Temple at Akashic Books, who continues to give voice to the voiceless.

SOUTHLAND
by Nina Revoyr
348 pages, trade paperback original, $15.95
*A *Los Angeles Times* Best-seller
*Winner of Lambda, Ferro-Grumley, and ALA's Stonewall Honor awards.

"What makes a book like *Southland* resonate is that it merges elements of literature and social history with the propulsive drive of a mystery, while evoking Southern California as a character, a key player in the tale. Such aesthetics have motivated other Southland writers, most notably Walter Mosley."
—*Los Angeles Times Book Review*

SONG FOR NIGHT
by Chris Abani
164 pages, trade paperback original, $12.95

"Chris Abani might be the most courageous writer working right now. There is no subject matter he finds daunting, no challenge he fears. Aside from that, he's stunningly prolific and writes like an angel. If you want to get at the molten heart of contemporary fiction, Abani is the starting point."
—Dave Eggers, author of *What Is the What*

SHE'S GONE
by Kwame Dawes
340 pages, trade paperback original, $15.95

"Dawes captures the sodden heat and beauty of the Caribbean with ease [and] infuses the story with the flavors, poetry, and rhythms of reggae music. He obviously loves the music and lets it shine in his characters and story, along with his adoration of Jamaica . . . As a love letter to Jamaica, *She's Gone* has beautiful moments."
—*Time Out Chicago*